"Rose," he yelled nny O'Flaherty from

He walked to the back where another door led to a small yard. "Rose," he called, knocking.

Puzzled, he looked around, but there was no sign of anyone. At the side of the house was a vegetable garden. The rows of potatoes and onions had been carefully hoed and weeded.

A raven croaked at him from a squat bush. Then, something sticking from behind a mound of dried turf caught his eye. He looked carefully. It was a boot. One of those boots people called Wellingtons. Danny walked over to the pile of turf and looked behind it.

What he saw took his breath away. An old woman lay sprawled on the ground, her head in a puddle of fresh blood. She wore a blue housedress and the Wellingtons. Her hair was gray and her right arm was twisted up underneath her. Beside her was a *slane*, a turf spade, its blade spattered with blood.

---
★
---

*Forthcoming from Worldwide Mystery by*
*JONATHAN HARRINGTON*

THE SECOND SORROWFUL MYSTERY

# Jonathan Harrington

# the Death of Cousin Rose

## WORLDWIDE®

TORONTO • NEW YORK • LONDON
AMSTERDAM • PARIS • SYDNEY • HAMBURG
STOCKHOLM • ATHENS • TOKYO • MILAN
MADRID • WARSAW • BUDAPEST • AUCKLAND

**THE DEATH OF COUSIN ROSE**

A Worldwide Mystery/May 2000

First published by Write Way Publishing, Inc.

ISBN 0-373-26347-3

**Printed in U.S.A.**

# ONE

THE DAY HE buried his father, Danny O'Flaherty booked a flight to Ireland.

Nine months later he arrived at Shannon Airport on a bright and chilly morning, flying nonstop from New York, and rented a Ford Escort. At a bend in the road outside of the village of Sixmilebridge he pulled over and got out of the car. The fields were littered with boulders and crisscrossed with stone walls, creating a patchwork of small farms. One crumbling wall held back a shaggy herd of sheep. A gravel drive led up from the main road to a whitewashed cottage; the smell of burning turf and cow dung lingered in the air. The sun, which had cast a golden spell over the scene a moment before, suddenly disappeared behind a cloud and mist rolled over the mountain.

Danny felt a surge of emotion. He drew a deep breath, thinking for a moment of Ireland: her lakes and hills; her fog-shrouded peaks and valleys; her tragic history.

Danny got back into the car. It felt strange getting behind the wheel on the right-hand side and pulling out onto the "wrong" side of the road. He awkwardly handled the stick shift on the rental car, turned on to N-68 and continued west through a series of small villages: Dairagh, Bansha, Lissy-casey, Knockalough, Goulbourne, Tullagower, Moyadda—little more than crossroads, where thatch-roofed Irish cottages stood derelict beside new government-built bungalows.

Occasionally, a farmer would cross the road with a pack of sheep behind him, or a John Deere tractor pulling a wagon-load of silage would force Danny to slow to an excruciating pace. Driving past these small farms and stone walls of west Clare, Danny was anxious to get to Ballycara.

When he passed through Kilrush and the seaside village of Kilkee, Danny was frantic with antici-pation. He was tempted to stop at a pub for a Guin-ness Stout, but decided to wait until he got to Car-rigaholt, or Ballycara itself. He did stop for petrol, which cost almost $5.00 a gallon. That came as a shock to Danny, who had inherited his father's par-simonious nature. The fact that the Irish Imperial gallon was slightly larger than the American gallon was of little consolation and he winced as he saw the meter turn over. To put it bluntly, Danny O'Flaherty was a cheapskate.

Outside of Kilkee, the road narrowed consider-ably and was split, cracked, and filled with pot-holes. He slowed the car to a crawl for part of the way. Low stone cottages with thatched roofs sat on both sides of the road in sharp contrast to the occasional modern ranch-style home.

The road passed through the center of a small collection of houses. Rainwater stood in puddles in the street and the facades of the houses were worn and cracked from the harsh salt air. A bicycle leaned against a wall.

The street was deserted but for an unsteady gentleman who made his way carefully to the other side and entered a low building with a neon Harp Lager sign in the window. A hand-painted sign over the door read: LARKIN'S PUB. At the end of the street stood a two-story building, freshly painted a cheerful green with mustard-colored trim.

This was Ballycara, where Danny's grandfather O'Flaherty was born.

Danny slowed the car to take stock of Ballycara. He noticed a curtain pull away slightly from behind a window and he sensed he was being watched by a hundred pairs of eyes. A young man came out of Larkin's Pub and Danny leaned his head out the car window.

"I'm looking for Mrs. Slattery's," he said to the young man.

"I'm after coming from there myself. Sure, isn't it just below."

"What?" Danny asked. The youth's brogue was so thick Danny thought for a moment he was speaking Gaelic. "How's that?"

The young man laughed good-naturedly. "So it's a holiday you're on, is it? Mrs. Slattery's the green one just there."

Danny had caught the words "Slattery" and "green," so he thanked the young man and put the car in gear.

"I'm Brendan Grady," the youth offered. "You must be the Yank."

"Yeah. I'm Danny O'Flaherty," he said, offering his hand.

"Grand to know you, Danny. When you're settled in, come on over to Larkin's and I'll stand you a pint."

"Thanks," Danny said, tentatively.

Danny parked in front of the green and yellow house. He let himself in through a wrought iron gate and made his way toward the back, where an elderly woman knelt in the garden, tending flowers. She was stooped slightly and had silver-gray hair. She wore a faded blue house dress and rubber Wellingtons.

"Mrs. Slattery," Danny said gently, so as not to startle her.

The woman looked up with a flower in her hand.

Mrs. Slattery smiled brightly and pushed a lock of hair away from her face with a gloved hand. "Danny O'Flaherty, you're welcome," she said, and led him inside beside a turf fire.

Although the house had been modernized, it still

maintained a traditional decor. Above the fireplace was a stone mantle. On the mantle was a picture of the Sacred Heart of Jesus and across the room hung a portrait of Pope John XXIII and, oddly, beside the Holy Father was a framed portrait of Elvis Presley. On the opposite wall was a cross made of reeds. This was St. Bridget's Cross, Danny would later learn, believed by Irish country people to protect the house. A new cross was made every year for St. Bridget's Feast on February first.

Mrs. Slattery pulled a chair in front of the fire for Danny and turned toward the kitchen to make a pot of tea.

"So are you just after arriving, Danny?"

"Excuse me?"

"You're after arriving from Shannon, so?"

The woman's brogue was as incomprehensible as Brendan Grady's, but Danny caught the word Shannon and took it from there.

"My flight got in this morning at seven-thirty. But I feel rested, no jet lag. I've had my watch set ahead five hours for a week now, just to get used to Irish time."

"Sure, and what brings you to Ireland?" Mrs. Slattery asked.

Before Danny could answer, the tea-kettle began to whistle and Mrs. Slattery shuffled into the kitchen.

What did bring him here?

This was Danny's second trip to Ireland, although the first was no more than a hazy memory. When he was thirteen, Danny's mother brought him on a trip to Ireland. It was the fulfillment of the dream of a lifetime for her and a disappointment to Danny. The villages of Mayo, on the western coast where his mother's aunts, uncles, and cousins lived, seemed damp and cut off from the world. He'd found the Irish brogue difficult to understand, and his own American accent had been mocked by his numerous cousins.

When his mother died ten years later, Danny doubted he would ever go back to Ireland. But he thanked God she had gotten a chance to stand in her mother's kitchen and breathe the misty air of the Ireland she had heard so much about.

Then, nine months ago, Danny's father had passed away suddenly, of a heart attack. His father had been a mortician who lived alone in the family home above the O'Flaherty Funeral Parlor in Upper Manhattan. Danny had two older sisters who lived in New York, and four younger brothers who were spread throughout the country. As the oldest male, his father had always looked to Danny to take over the family business.

But Danny never wanted any part of it. After high school, when his father pressured him to take the mortuary science course and go into business with him, Danny fled the city and enrolled in college out of state.

After Danny got his degree he went back to New York, moved into a studio in Greenwich Village and began teaching at Our Lady Queen of Martyrs Catholic School.

When his father died Danny moved back to the family home above the funeral parlor. But the dusty memories of the apartment oppressed him, so the business was taken over by an associate of his father's.

Having never married, Danny was considered a good catch by the women in his parish. He had dated an English teacher, Sara Woods, but they had broken off soon after the death of Danny's father. Danny blamed it on himself, because he had become withdrawn and moody. He felt guilty for not taking up his father's trade, although he still didn't want to be an undertaker. In fact, corpses scared him.

Besides, the thought of settling down with Sara Woods—who would take care of their babies upstairs, while Danny embalmed corpses downstairs…was more than he could bear.

But the gathering of the family for his father's funeral, the Mass, the Rosary, and the final realization that both of his parents were dead, had put Danny in mind of his roots.

Unlike his mother, Danny's father had never

spoken of "the Old Country," and he rarely mentioned his parents, who'd died when Danny was quite young. Danny's Grandfather O'Flaherty had emigrated from County Clare just after World War I. Grandma O'Flaherty had also emigrated from Ireland but Danny did not know from which county. They had met in America, married and became citizens. Danny's father had always insisted, a bit shrilly, that now his parents "were Americans."

His father half-jokingly called his wife's people "shanty Irish," and his mother accused his father of being "lace curtain Irish." The O'Flahertys were not heavy drinkers, nor were they particularly fervent in their devotion to the Church. "A penny saved is a penny earned," might have been the maxim of his father's family.

At the funeral, Danny had asked his siblings what they could remember about their grandparents. His sisters had great stories of their mother's parents, but information about their father's parents was sketchy; Grandpa O'Flaherty had never talked about his roots. When he died in 1960 he still had the west Clare brogue, even though he had emigrated to America in 1919 or 1920.

"What town in Clare was he from?" Danny had asked.

"He never said," answered Danny's oldest sister, who had the clearest memory of their grandfather.

"Did he have brothers and sisters?"

"Yeah, there was one named Sean, I think."

"Did Sean live in Ireland?"

"Yeah, but he came to America once. I remember meeting him when I was just a little girl."

"Is he still alive?"

"If he is, he'd be an old man by now."

"What about Grandma O'Flaherty?"

"Oh, she died long before I was born. I never knew anything about her and I never heard Grandpa mention her."

"What about Dad? Did he ever talk about his mother?"

"She died when he was just a baby."

"Did they ever go back to Ireland?"

"Back to Ireland?" Danny's sister repeated, incredulously. "There was nothing for them back there; they were Americans."

The morning of his father's funeral Danny decided that he would go to Ireland the following summer. Images of his trip to Ireland with his mother came back to him often over the following year and he began to wonder more seriously about his father's family. Soon, Danny began a genealogical research in earnest. He focused on his Grandfather O'Flaherty. Danny wrote to the Department of Immigration and Naturalization to get a copy of his grandparents' naturalization papers. He received a certified copy of Grandma O'Flaherty's papers, but they could not locate a record for his grandfather. After that, he wrote to several shipping companies that had been engaged in the immigration trade and requested passenger lists for the years between 1910 and 1930 to see if his grandfather's name appeared on a list of passengers, but he had had no luck.

MRS. SLATTERY returned from the kitchen carrying a silver platter with a pot of tea, brown bread, and butter and jam on it, which she placed on a low table in front of the fire between her rocker and Danny's chair.

"You'll have some tea then and I'll show you to your room."

Danny took a cup of the steaming tea from Mrs. Slattery and a piece of the brown bread.

"No butter on your soda bread?"

"No, thanks."

Mrs. Slattery smiled. "Yanks," she said playfully. "I'll never understand them."

She took a sip of her tea. "So, you're digging up your roots, Danny?"

Danny's face flushed with embarrassment, though he wasn't sure why.

"Well, I knew your grandfather," Mrs. Slattery said.

"You did?" Danny was astonished. Somehow all his research had seemed so abstract: the Immigration and Nationalization Service records; the search through ship's registries; the 1910 census. So for this woman to calmly say she *knew* his grandfather was amazing. For Danny, his grandfather had become an historical figure, a footnote in ancient census documents.

"Sure, I was a wee bit of a thing." To Mrs. Slattery he was a person. "Your grandfather went out to the states just after the Easter Rebellion."

The Easter Rebellion, Mrs. Slattery explained, took place on Easter Monday, 1916. A group of Irishmen took over the General Post Office in Dublin and proclaimed Ireland a Republic, free of England. Seventeen of the Irish leaders were captured by the British and executed.

"What was he like?" Danny asked.

"Who?"

"My grandfather."

Mrs. Slattery put her tea cup on the tray and got up. "I was just a child when he emigrated. My father and your grandfather were in the Rebellion together."

"Really?"

"Ach, but that was years ago." Mrs. Slattery touched the side of her head. "Me memory doesn't serve me well, anymore."

She had a good memory for history, Danny

mused. She just didn't want to talk about his grandfather, it seemed.

"Come on with you," Mrs. Slattery said abruptly. "I'll show you to your room."

The room was simple, but comfortable. A narrow bed with an electric blanket; a crucifix hung above the bed; and on the opposite wall was a painting of St. Martin de Porres.

Danny hung his shirts in the worn wooden wardrobe that stood against one wall. On the door of the wardrobe was an antique mirror in a tarnished frame.

When Mrs. Slattery left the room, Danny looked into the mirror. He was thirty-nine years old. Flecks of gray salted his shock of black curls. He wore a mustache, which he kept neatly trimmed. Only a few traces of red in his mustache hinted at the Viking raids that had hit Ireland in the eighth century.

At six-foot-one, Danny was average by American standards—above average by Irish. His bushy eyebrows grew together over the bridge of his nose (like his grandfather's) and his brown eyes peered at his own reflection with a questioning gaze.

"Who am I, really?" he wondered.

# TWO

THE FLIGHT had taken its toll despite Danny's clever scheme for avoiding jet lag.

He picked up a local paper from the dresser before lying down to sleep and read outloud: "Mr. Colm Mulcahy of Doonbeg was fined thirty pounds and ordered to pay fifty pounds costs, when he was convicted of having under-sized oysters in his possession by Justice Patrick Casey."

Danny smiled. High crime area, he thought as he loosened his tie, lay down on the bed, and dropped off to sleep for the next six hours.

When he woke, he looked around dumbfounded. He swung his feet off the bed and rubbed his eyes. He focused on the picture of St. Martin on the wall across the room, remembering he was in Ireland.

Standing up unsteadily, he decided to go to the pub he had passed that morning. But he should call Rose, he admonished himself, and let her know he had arrived. He wanted to see her in the morning. Rose was his main contact in Ireland.

When Danny's research into his father's family had turned up nothing, he had put a personal ad in a column called "Absent Friends" in *Ireland's Own*, a magazine published in Wexford.

"Danny O'Flaherty is trying to find out something about his grandfather, Daniel P. O'Flaherty, who emigrated to America from County Clare around 1919-1920. He was known to have one brother named Sean. Danny would be pleased to hear from anyone who can give information about his grandfather. Reply to 56 207th St., Apt 10B, New York, NY 10040."

That's how Danny O'Flaherty met Rose Noonan.

Just before Christmas, Danny received a letter from Ireland. He examined the colorful stamp with the word "Eire" printed on it, and ripped opened the envelope excitedly.

Ballycara
County Clare
Ireland

Dear Mr. O'Flaherty,
I saw your annoucement in *Ireland's Own* recently, bearing your name and address and stating that Daniel P. O'Flaherty was your grandfather. I am Rose Noonan (nee

O'Flaherty) a niece of Daniel P. O'Flaherty being the only child of Sean O'Flaherty (brother to Daniel). My father Sean died in 1945. The homestead from which your grandfather emigrated in 1920 is now closed down. If you ever come to Ireland, I would gladly show you the old home place and introduce you to some of your cousins in the area. I have some information about your grandfather that I think you would find very interesting.

May God bless and keep you,
Rose O'Flaherty Noonan

At last he knew where his grandfather had been born. He had taken down his map of Ireland and searched through County Clare for the town of Ballycara. It sat by the mouth of the Shannon river on the north side of a crooked finger of land that poked into the Atlantic—The Loop Head Peninsula.

Just seeing the name of the village on a map had been enough to send Danny's mind racing. He was more excited than ever about seeing Ballycara and the house where his grandfather was born and had lived in until he'd emigrated. He finalized his travel plans soon after receiving Rose's letter. When he replied he had written playfully that he would be coming in June—''when summer's in the meadow.'' Later, he regretted it, thinking that was just the kind of maudlin stuff the Irish hated.

Rose had written back giving him explicit directions to her house from Ballycara. In response to his questions about accommodations she wrote that he was welcome to stay with her, but if he insisted on a hotel, he would have to stay at Mrs. Slattery's Bed and Breakfast since it was the only place in Ballycara that rented rooms.

And at last he was here.

DANNY WALKED DOWN the stairs. Mrs. Slattery was not to be seen. Probably in the garden, Danny thought.

Outside the pub was a green, wooden telephone booth: TELEFON. Danny dug into his pockets and examined the unfamiliar coins. All the coins had a harp, the date, and EIRE on one side. The 20-pence coin had a stallion on the other side; the 10-pence coin had a fish; the 5-pence coin had a bull; and the one-pence coin had a peacock. The telephone itself was no less confusing.

Danny spread the paper out with his cousin's number on it and read the instructions for the phone. There was a little slot that you put the coins in. It was more like a ramp. You were to dial the number first, then there were two buttons, A and B. When the person answered you were to push button A. The coins rolled down the little ramp and disappeared into the phone. Danny fumbled awkwardly with the system until finally, after ten tries, he got through to his cousin. He could hear her, but she couldn't hear him. Frustrated, he pushed button B, which gave his coins back and terminated the call.

"Jesus Christ," he muttered in exasperation and tried again. Four or five tries later he miraculously got through. "This is Danny O'Flaherty," he yelled as if he were calling from America.

"Danny, I'm so anxious to see you. Was your flight comfortable?"

"Yes. It was fine."

"I hope you'll be out tomorrow then. I've got a lot to tell you about your grandfather."

"I'm looking forward to it," Danny said, and they chatted for awhile. "I'll see you tomorrow morning about ten."

"Yes, indeed. I've got some important information for you."

WHEN DANNY OPENED the door of Larkin's Pub, four pairs of eyes examined him through the semidarkness. A turf fire burning in the fireplace emitted a pleasant glow of warmth.

Danny recognized Brendan Grady, the young fellow he had met that morning.

"Danny," Brendan called out, motioning him over to the fire where he sat with two other men.

"Bring your man here a jar, Seamus," he called to the publican, Seamus Larkin.

The publican slapped a wet rag on the bar and wiped angrily. "Sure and who's paying for it?"

"I'm paying, Seamus, I'm paying!" Brendan shot back, but in a friendly tone. "This here's the Yank, Danny O'Flaherty. His grandda was from Ballycara."

The publican looked at Danny suspiciously. But Brendan Grady carried on in a friendly tone. "Danny, this is Tim Mahoney. He's our resident archaeologist. Teaches English and Religion up at the school, when he's not here. But if you're interested in fairy rings, ring forts, stone forts, passage graves, dolmons, you know, all that old stuff, he's your man."

"'Tis a pleasure," said Tim, shaking Danny's hand warmly. He was a good-sized fellow with a mop of curly brown hair and a square jaw.

Seamus Larkin continued to eye Danny suspiciously as he scraped the heads off the pints of Guinness with a spatula and set them on the drain board to settle.

"And this is Liam Flynn," Brendan said, indicating the elderly man sitting beside them in front of the fire. His skin was wrinkled and swarthy and his stringy black hair was slicked back over his head. He puffed eagerly on a pipe and spat into the fire. "God bless you, son," he said, extending a calloused hand.

"Liam lives beside your cousin, Rose," Brendan said.

"Oh, really?" Again, Danny was taken back. "You live beside my cousin?"

"Yes, damn her," said Liam with a laugh. "I've been trying to get that rocky farm of hers for nearly half a century."

Seamus set three pints of Guinness in front of the men. A brief altercation ensued as the three men haggled halfheartedly over the right to pay. In the end, Danny somehow got stuck with it and grudgingly handed over a ten-pound note.

Liam Flynn sipped his stout, smacked his lips and continued. "Sure, she wouldn't marry me and by God she won't sell it to me."

All three of the men laughed.

"What's a fellow to do?" he added, spitting into the fire.

Seamus snarled from behind the bar. "Take care of your own place a little better and stop coveting your neighbor's property. That is what a fellow's to do."

"Jesus, Mary, and Joseph," cried Brendan. "Will you listen to Seamus? Sure, he's as righteous as Father O'Malley. And I suppose ye'll be hearing confession after closing."

"If you worked harder," Seamus shot back,

"and worried less about what the other fellow's got, you'd make out a lot better in the end." The publican wiped the bar furiously. "Look at me. I worked fifteen years in bloody England. Saved every pound I made. Sent as much as I could home to Mother. Still, I had enough to come back and buy this pub."

The men sipped their stout and Danny looked around the pub. Now that his eyes had adjusted to the gloom, he felt warm and comfortable in the spartan room, despite the unfriendly bartender.

Seamus stood behind the rough wooden bar polishing glasses while the three men stared into the fire.

"Did you know my grandfather?" Danny asked Liam Flynn.

"Well, of course I did. My father was with him in this very pub the day your grandda left for America."

"What was he like?" Danny asked. "You know, my grandfather."

"Sure, shouldn't you know your own grandfather better than I would?"

"I was only a child, five or six years old, when he died."

"Well, I'm sure he was a great man to go out to the states from this place."

"Is there anyone else alive who would remember him?"

Tim Mahoney spoke up. "Most of the old folk are dead, really. There were two people here now, Johnny Welsh and Sonny Murphy, who would have lots and lots of stories about your grandda. But they're dead now too, God rest their souls."

Liam Flynn blessed himself and took a sip of stout.

"Is there any way to find out what year my grandfather was born and the names of his parents?"

"Digging up your bloody roots, are you?" The publican hissed contemptuously across the room.

"And sure what if he is?" Brendan shot back. "Isn't it a fine thing to be interested in?"

"Have you checked the records of the church?" Liam asked. "I'm sure Father O'Malley would gladly show you the records."

"Better keep an eye out for that one," Brendan said, winking. "He'll be looking for something in the collection plate as well."

Liam took his pipe from his mouth. "Watch your tongue when you speak of the clergy."

"The bleeding clergy," Brendan began angrily, "have just about ruined this godforsaken country."

Danny was finding it hard keeping the company focused on the topic of his grandfather.

"Tell me something, Brendan. Didn't your family have a bit of a quarrel with Daniel?"

"Sure, that was years ago," Brendan said.

"And I remember one of ye saying once that you never let an old quarrel die."

Danny was intrigued. "Quarrel?"

Brendan Grady made a motion toward the publican to shut him up, but Seamus raised his voice. "Sure, didn't it have something to do with your bloody Republican principles?"

It was believed in the region that Brendan Grady had ties to the outlawed Provisional Wing of the Irish Republican Army. His family had been staunch Republicans for generations and an uncle of his was interred at Long Kesh during the Civil Rights movement in Belfast in the 1960s. Brendan was known to disappear for weeks at a time for unknown reasons. Some believed he was on active maneuvers with the IRA. He made no secret of his support for Sinn Fein, the political party of the IRA, and of his hatred of the British, although the recent IRA cease-fire had taken the wind out of his sails.

"What would you know about principles, Seamus Larkin?"

"As I remember the story," Seamus continued, "this young Danny's grandfather and your grandfather were partners."

"'Tis true," conceded Brendan. "When the treaty was signed in nineteen twenty-one and the so-called Free State of Ireland was created, the true sons of Ireland fought against the traitors who had signed away the six counties of the North to the Brits.''

Danny knew well the history of the Irish Civil War. Although the Easter Rebellion had failed, it stirred up the Irish and eventually led to the treaty, making the twenty-six counties in the south a Republic free of Britain. But the six counties of the north were left to Britain. Those satisfied with the treaty supported the newly formed Republic of Ireland. But the Irish Republican Army insisted that they would never stop fighting until *all* of Ireland was free.

''Your grandfather,'' Brendan pointed his finger at Danny, ''sided with the Free Staters and my grandfather died in the glorious service of the Irish Republican Army.''

''Bunch of bloody thugs,'' the publican spat.

''True heroes of Ireland,'' shouted Liam Flynn, banging his glass on the table.

''Probably a bit of both,'' offered Tim Mahoney, always the diplomat. ''Besides, if the peace process continues, we might see the end of the troubles in our lifetimes.''

''Peace process,'' Brendan spat out, as if it were a curse.

Danny sensed that there was more to the story than Brendan was revealing. He also sensed that this was not a topic to be taken up lightly in the company of these men—especially the publican, who seemed to be a trouble maker.

"Sure and what was it," the publican seemed determined to stir up controversy, "that the boy's grandfather did, exactly, to earn the wrath of the Grady clan for all these years?"

Brendan took a sip of stout and inhaled deeply. "Well, it began just after the treaty was signed—"

Suddenly the door of the pub rattled open, letting in a draft of wet, chilly air. A slender, nervous-looking whippet poked its nose tentatively into the pub, then stepped in, followed by a tall, gangly gentleman.

Danny smiled at the resemblance between the dog and its owner. The whippet, a greyhound type, had a sharp angular snout, skin pulled tight over its ribs, and a sandy-gray complexion. Its master was over six feet, thin, angular, with a protruding Adam's apple, and gray hair.

"After a bit of hare coursing, Mr. Pinkerton?" the publican called, fawningly.

Brendan Grady's mouth twisted into a grimace. "Mister," he muttered into his jar.

Pinkerton commanded his dog to sit and the whippet dutifully dropped to its haunches in the middle of the room. "Indeed, and there wasn't a hare in sight all day. Do you suppose it's the weather?"

Grady guffawed and winked at Danny.

"You know it's bad luck to kill a hare before sunrise," old Liam Flynn offered.

"Yes, so they say," Pinkerton returned, a note of condescension in his voice.

Liam Flynn sucked his pipe noisily and added, "Some of the lads believe, and I'm not saying I'm one of them, that witches take the form of hares so they can get into the fields and cast a spell over the cattle."

"Yes, well…" Pinkerton began, then turned abruptly to the publican. "Give me a bottle of Jameson if you will."

"Too good to drink with the likes of us," Brendan whispered to Danny, who was still having trouble understanding the heavily-accented conversation. He had just figured out that "hare coursing" was rabbit hunting in some form. Probably with the dog.

"Here you are, Mr. Pinkerton," the publican said, handing the bottle to the tall man.

Pinkerton snapped his fingers and the dog jumped to its feet and looked around nervously.

"Good evening, lads," Pinkerton said as he stepped out of the pub, followed by his dog.

"Good evening, sir," cried Seamus.

When the door slammed behind him, Brendan Grady mimicked the publican. "Good evening, sir, Mr. Pinkerton. Can I kiss your arse for you, Lord Pinkerton."

"He spends more in this bloody pub than you," Seamus said hotly. "And I don't have to listen to the fookin' palaver from him that comes out of you."

Danny was astonished. "You mean there are *still* lords around here?"

Tim Mahoney, who had been the quietest of the trio, spoke up. "That man is as Irish as the rest of us here, Danny."

"Fookin' Protestant," Brendan muttered.

Liam Flynn raised a finger at Brendan. "Sure, I've known some mighty fine Protestant people. Wolfe Tone himself was a Protestant, or have you forgotten your history?"

Danny had not. Wolfe Tone was an Irish Protestant barrister who believed in equality for Catholics and Protestants. In 1791, he'd founded the Society of United Irishmen, which championed civil rights for Catholics and independence for Ireland. Danny did find it amusing that two hundred years later Wolfe Tone's name was still dropped as if he had been in yesterday's paper.

Tim Mahoney left the two to argue as he explained to Danny, "Mr. Pinkerton lives in the manor house out in the direction of your cousin's place. Trelawny it's called…the estate. It's been in Pinkerton's family for over two hundred years. Jeremiah Pinkerton was an Englishman. That man you just saw, George Pinkerton, is Jeremiah's eldest son's only son's elder son's elder son. It's through primogeniture that he has the estate. He's a decent lad and as Irish as the rest of us.'' Primogeniture: the system by which land is passed down through the generations to the oldest son, Danny thought. ''Would you like to go out and see the ring fort on the grounds?'' Mahoney finished.

Danny was enthusiastic. ''Sure.''

Brendan Grady was livid. ''As Irish as the rest of us? His forebearers drove the Irish off that land. And in the famine times, when the Irish were dying by the millions, did the Pinkertons suffer at all, tell me! Irish my arse. It's the likes of his kind that put the Irish in the shape we're in today. And let me tell you something: I don't give a damn about this bloody peace process. No agreement with the British is worth the paper it's written on.''

''For the love of God, Brendan,'' old Liam spoke up. ''Let bygones be bygones.''

Seamus came over with a few bricks of turf and tossed them into the fireplace.

Tim Mahoney noted Danny's curiosity and explained: ''Turf, you see, is what we use instead of coal, although its only half as potent. We cut the turf out on the bog.''

Danny had finished three pints of Guinness. He was having such a grand time he'd hardly noticed the time going by. But when he stood up to go to the bathroom—the toilet, as the Irish called it—his legs felt rubbery beneath him.

He walked carefully to the back of the pub. Against the back wall, just out of sight of the rest of the pub, a gutter ran along the floor. Danny did not know what it was until he caught the acrid stench and saw old Liam Flynn swaying above it, pissing a stream of stout.

Danny took care of his business and returned to the main room of the pub. Brendan Grady had launched into a song *a cappella* in a decent tenor voice.

Another pint of Guinness was sitting on the low table at Danny's place by the fire when he got there. He took a deep drink, belched politely, and leaned back with a smile of satisfaction. The warm glow he felt from his toenails to the top of his head was more than just the Guinness doing its job; Danny felt a sense of belonging he rarely felt in his own country. These men were like brothers to him. They *were* brothers, Danny philosophized, taking another drink of stout. He wiped the creamy foam from his mustache and imagined his grandfather in this setting.

He had only dim memories of his grandfather. The old man must have been in his eighties, and Danny no more than six or seven. What he remembered was an old man, sitting in the living room of his parents' home, fanning himself and muttering about the heat. Danny remembered carrying a shotglass of whiskey to him, walking carefully so as not to spill it. That was about all he remembered, a tiny glass in his tiny hands, handing it up to an old man who smelled of pipe smoke.

A year later his grandfather was dead. Danny had hardly given another thought to his grandfather until the day his own father died, thirty-three years later. Then, all of a sudden, he wanted to know everything there was to know about his grandfather.

"Are you having another pint, Danny?" Tim Mahoney asked as he finished off his.

Danny felt a bit bloated. "I better not."

"Sure, have another pint," Tim coaxed.

"Well, make up your minds quick," Seamus called from behind the bar. "It's nearly half-eleven now."

Just then the door rattled again and a short man in the uniform of the *Garda Siochana,* the Irish Police, with carrot-colored hair and a drooping red mustache, stuck his head into the pub.

"It's almost time, Seamus," he called into the pub.

"I'm after calling last round now," Seamus yelled back. "Come in and meet the Yank."

The garda stepped halfway in. "I heard there was a holiday-maker in town. Since he's an

O'Flaherty, he'll know I run a tight ship. No black-guards wanted in these parts.''

"Oh, come in," said Brendan Grady. "We're just having a bit of the *craic*."

Danny looked at him. "Crack?" he asked, astonished.

"Good times, Danny. Fun."

"Oh, I see," Danny said, laughing and repeating the word.

"So you're Danny O'Flaherty. I'm Garda Donal Kelley," the garda said with self-importance.

"Pleased to meet you."

"I'm after talking to Mrs. Slattery. The woman's a saint, God love her," he said. "You're staying at Shannonside?"

"Yes."

"How long will you be here?"

"Just ten days," Danny said a little sadly, already regretting that he would be leaving so soon.

"Well, I'll tolerate no cod in this town, nor put up with blackguards."

There was something slightly comic about Garda Kelley, Danny thought. The man was no more than five feet three and shaped like a barrel from the neck down. Atop the barrel rested his large squarish head, and his reddish ears stuck out sharply, like a pair of wings. His eyeglasses had been out of style in the states since the 1950s.

"You'll have no trouble from me," Danny said,

surprising himself by the slight brogue he was developing. He smiled and hoisted his glass. "Sure, I'm just here for the *craic*."

"Well, finish your jars, boys," the garda said. "It's nearly half-eleven."

"Won't you have one with us, Donal?" asked Seamus.

"Now, you know I never drink on duty, Seamus. I don't know why you ask questions like that."

"Ah, just one while I close up."

Garda Kelley looked greedily at the pint of stout in front of Danny as if struggling with himself to keep control. He turned on the publican suddenly. "I said drink up," he shouted. "You know I tolerate no blackguards here." He pointed accusingly at Danny. "You remember that too, Yank."

Danny shot a glance at Brendan as if to ask: *Is this guy for real?*

Garda Kelley turned and marched out of the pub.

"You heard him, lads," said Seamus. "Drink up."

But no one made a move to finish.

At 11:30, Seamus closed the curtains on the window that faced the street, bolted the door, turned off the lights, drew himself a Murphy's stout and pulled up a chair to the fire.

Tim Mahoney raised his pint in the air. His ruddy face blazed in the firelight. *"Sláinte,"* he said, tipping his glass toward Danny. "To the Yank."

Danny smiled.

"*Sláinte*," the rest chorused. "To the Yank!"

Brendan Grady winked at him. "Welcome home, Danny Boy."

# THREE

DANNY WOKE EARLY, with a bitter taste like copper in his mouth, and a head that throbbed slightly. Yet beneath the dull hangover was a feeling of euphoria.

Swinging out of bed, he pulled the faded lace curtains aside and opened the window. A gust of cool air smelling of salt blew in from the sea. Screeching gulls twirled overhead, then disappeared behind Larkin's Pub. To the west the fog dissipated slightly. Danny could barely make out the distant cliffs that plunged into the Atlantic.

He thought again for a moment of his father's parents. Danny pictured his grandpa in 1919:

*Dan O'Flaherty stood on a cliff overlooking the slate-blue ocean. Back in his parents' cottage he had packed what few belongings he owned. The rain had momentarily abated and the air was scented with the smoke of turf fires. He drew a deep breath and looked out over the bay to the thin line of the horizon that lay like a length of twine between the sea and the rising moon. He tried to imagine that the full moon itself was the*

*New World to the west. In fact, the moon seemed closer. There at the edge of the bay he thought that if he could reach out he could touch it—that new world, America. How distant it was! But soon his ship, bound for New York Harbor, would depart from Galway.*

*Daniel thought of all that was behind him—the whole of Ireland: her lakes and hills; her fog-shrouded peaks and valleys; her rain; her starving children of the bog.*

*He did not love Ireland. How could he? For seven years, since he was fifteen, he had labored to wrench a living from these cruel, rocky acres of the Western World. His father had farmed twelve acres, which would go to his brother Sean when the old man died. There was no use waiting for that day; he would have to emigrate. He was ready to go.*

*Not that he had not made every effort to remain. But the rains had ruined his crop for the third consecutive year. Finally, he'd thrown up his hands, and to his mother had said: "T'hell with it. I'll go to America."*

*"What shall you do in America, then?"*

*"I'll go to Uncle Michael's in Chicago," he'd said.*

*Daniel's uncle Michael had gone to work for a pipe-fitting company in Chicago and was said to be doing well.*

*His mother had been hurt; her son was leaving home. Her two sons had lived their entire lives on this lonely farm at the foot of a hill overlooking the sea. She would miss him sorely.*

*And then he left, never to return.*

THE TEA KETTLE whistled downstairs in Mrs. Slattery's kitchen and Danny woke up in the present. Could his grandfather have even imagined that a grandson of his would come back to this same rocky shore, to dig among cemetery stones overgrown with mosses and ferns, searching for the names of his ancestors? Could he have ever understood that just as Daniel P. O'Flaherty had fled from this land to escape its damp and misty past, his grandchildren would come back through the mist with passenger lists, civil records, and data gleaned from old census reports, to recapture that very past?

Downstairs, when Danny broached the subject over a breakfast of eggs, sausage, rashers, fried tomatoes, and tea, Mrs. Slattery put it best. "Who would have thought," she said of those who had emigrated, "that there would be so much research into their coming and going? Sure, when they left they thought that was the end of them and no one would think about them again."

Danny agreed, and pushing at the sausage on his plate, asked: "What's this?"

Mrs. Slattery laughed. "Sure, a Yank wouldn't know *drisheen,* I don't suppose?"

*"Drisheen?"* Danny laughed nervously and put a forkful of the sausage in his mouth, chewing tentatively.

"It's pig's blood," she said good-naturedly. "Coagulated pig's blood."

Danny gagged, forcing himself not to show his disgust. He swallowed the disagreeable lump and washed it down with tea. "Tasty," he offered, with a weak smile.

"Here, have some more," Mrs. Slattery said, and Danny watched with dismay as she scooped more *drisheen* onto his plate.

"Why did most of them emigrate?" he asked her, thinking it was probably the food that drove them out of Ireland.

"It wasn't easy living on the bits of farms people had in West Clare. Isn't so you'd make a living at all, but you'd exist."

"I see."

"You're off to see your cousin, Rose, so?"

"Yeah. Thought I'd drive out there this morning."

"Tell her I'll be taking good care of you here at Shannonside."

"I will."

"I'm thinking you'd want to stop at Killballyowen Cemetery where your great-grandparents are buried.''

"You bet," Danny said excitedly. "Where's that?"

"Sure, it's just below Cross on the left. Now your grandfather would have gone to the old school in Cross. Your great-grandfather's grave is the first one on the right, just inside the gate. My own father, God rest his soul, is buried there, too.''

After breakfast, Danny started the car and headed out of Ballycara. He took the long way through Rahona, Cloonconeen (on Rinevella Bay), Rehy Hill, then turned back toward Cross. Cross was no more than a few abandoned cottages and the ruins of the old school.

It had begun to drizzle slightly. Danny pulled the car over, got out, tugged his jacket tighter around him, and pushed open the rusted gate. Water stood in puddles in the muddy yard. Directly in front of him, a decaying white building of mortar stood with a plaque embedded in the wall indicating that this had been the Cross school.

The rain increased its tempo and Danny shivered slightly. He shivered not merely from the cold, but from the odd feeling of being in the presence of ghosts. Here in this school-yard his grandfather had played with his mates, oblivious to his destiny to emigrate and begin life again in a foreign land. All those children were long since dead, but Danny imagined their shouts echoing on the abandoned playground.

Danny stood transfixed among the ruins of the school until his shoes began to fill with water. He turned and rushed back to the car, flipped on the wipers, and drove on in the rain.

Despite the weather (or because of it) the scenery was beautiful. Although the road itself was a narrow, gutted track, rich green grasses grew beside it, and hedgerows crowded the road in places. Turning a curve beyond Feeard, the Atlantic glittered like an aluminum disk. For a moment the rain stopped and a ray of light shimmered on the sea. On both sides of the road, small farms separated by stone walls created a quilt of greenery. As Danny drove, the rain abated and he saw the abandoned cottages from which emigrants like his grandfather had fled. In most of the cabins, the thatch roofs had collapsed and fallen in, while in others the roof had gone to seed and sprouted thick patches of grass. The stone walls on the cottages had collapsed and some were no more than standing chimneys.

Danny knew from his books that this part of Ireland had suffered horribly from the famine. Between 1845 and 1850 the potato crops failed. Nearly one million Irish had starved to death, and an additional million had emigrated.

But that was over half a century before his grandfather emigrated.

Danny continued driving, slicking his rain-soaked hair off his forehead and looking out for the cemetery that was supposed to be on the left. There were some cottages still inhabited. Mounds of black turf were stacked beside the houses and occasionally Danny would see an old man working outside. One old fellow was driving a pack of sheep across the road. He wore a threadbare, but well-made, three-piece suit. Danny smiled. He could not imagine a farmer back in the States doing chores in a suit.

For the most part, however, the countryside was bleak and melancholy, yet beautiful in its haunting wildness. Suddenly, Danny spotted a small cemetery on the left side of the road. The rain had softened to a fine mist that clung to Danny's clothes and fogged his glasses as he stepped out of the car.

To his surprise, there was a young woman in the cemetery placing flowers on a grave. She appeared to be in her early thirties. She was red-cheeked, with shoulder-length red hair; she held a bunch of wildflowers in her hand.

Danny avoided looking at her as he searched among the stones for the O'Flaherty grave. Just inside the gate, he looked to the right. There were numerous upright stones, topped with Celtic crosses, and other flat markers overgrown with grass and covered with lichens. The inscriptions were worn away and Danny got down on his hands and knees to read them. The ground was soggy and the rain had begun to fall again. Danny ran his fingers over the wet stones. Finally, he found a flat, gray marker engulfed in grass. He pulled the grass away and could barely make out the inscription:

ERECTED BY DANIEL O'FLAHERTY,
BALLYCARA
IN LOVING MEMORY
OF HIS WIFE MARY
WHO DIED JULY 31, 1908
AGED 60 YEARS

Danny recorded the information in a notebook he kept in his jacket pocket and stood up. This would be his great-grandmother's grave. But where was his great-grandfather buried?

The rain was falling in earnest now, and the young woman stood beside her bicycle under the cover of a tree.

Danny walked over to where she stood. "Hello."

"'Tis a soft day," she remarked in a lilting brogue that made Danny's heart skip a beat.

He laughed. "It is soft all right. Why don't we go sit in the car?"

The woman's face went scarlet and Danny wondered what he'd said to embarrass her.

"You're the Yank, so?"

"That's right."

She laughed nervously and looked away.

"C'mon," Danny said, starting toward the car, "let's get out of this rain."

Danny loped across the cemetery toward the car. He opened the driver's side and looked back, but the woman had not moved. "C'mon, you'll get wet!" he shouted, then climbed in.

She stayed under the tree even as the rain increased. Danny opened the window and shouted again, "C'mon, it's pouring."

Reluctantly she made a move toward the car and Danny reached over and opened the passenger side. As the rain fell with increasing fury, the woman moved slowly, reluctantly, toward the car. Finally, as if suddenly making up her mind, she dashed to the car, stepped in, and slammed the door shut.

Danny pulled his glasses off and wiped them on his shirt. "This rain's driving me nuts," he said.

The woman laughed shyly.

When Danny put his glasses back on he could see even more clearly how beautiful she was. Her face glistened from rainwater, and her bright red hair had puffed up into curls from the humidity, framing her lightly freckled face in ringlets.

"If Father O'Malley hears about this, may the Lord have mercy on me," she said.

"What?"

"Father O'Malley..."

"What about him?"

The woman giggled nervously. "I suppose back in America a woman can sit in your car any time she feels like it."

"I see," Danny murmured, realizing that he had overstepped some imagined bounds of propriety. "Any time it's raining," he answered smartly.

The woman burst into good-natured laughter.

Danny stuck out his hand, which she shook awkwardly. "I'm Danny O'Flaherty."

"I know," she said. "I'm Fidelma Muldoon."

"I was looking for the grave of my great-grandparents," Danny said suddenly.

"And you found it, I see."

"Well, just my great-grandmother. I don't know where my great-grandfather is buried."

"There, under the same flag," said Fidelma. "No one added his name to it."

"How do you know?"

Fidelma laughed. "We don't know much around Ballycara, but we do know what happened to our own. Sure, there might not have been money to add your great-grandfather's name. Sometimes, those who went to America and made big money would send back enough for a fine monument.

Like that one,'' she said, pointing to the tallest Celtic cross in the graveyard. ''Jimmy Sweeney had the money sent back for his parents' marker there.''

''Maybe I should at least have his name added to the stone.''

'''Twould be nice.''

''But I don't know what year he died.''

''Come 'round to the church tomorrow and we'll have a look at the records.''

''Yes, I had intended to do that. Do you work there?''

''Aye. I'm Father O'Malley's housekeeper.''

''I see.'' For some reason the news disappointed Danny. He looked out the window. The rain had stopped and the sky was clearing to the west.

''I'll be going, so,'' Fidelma said.

Danny got out and opened the car door for her. He cast about in his mind for a way to prolong the meeting. ''So, what's the proper way around here,'' he asked suddenly, ''to take a young woman out in the car?''

Fidelma smiled. ''I'm thinking you'd want to bring her to a more cheerful place than a graveyard.''

''How about a drive up to the cliffs of Moher?''

'''Twould be lovely.''

''Tomorrow after we look at the records?''

Fidelma got on her bike, tossed her hair away from her face, and shoved off. "Perhaps."

As she pedaled away Danny shouted, "See you tomorrow, then."

But she rode on without answering.

Danny got back in the car and continued driving. After a while he could see Kilbaha Bay to his left. He passed a white, two-story building with a slate roof, and a sign outside that read:


KEATINGS:
HAVE ONE FOR THE ROAD
THE NEAREST BAR TO NEW YORK


Although the Loop Head Peninsula did jut far out to the west, Danny had his doubts as to whether this was the nearest bar to New York. He was tempted to stop in and argue the point over a jar of stout, but decided against it. He was watching his pence.

Danny saw a Tinker's wagon beside the road. He remembered the brightly-painted horse-drawn wagons that the Tinkers had driven when Danny had first come to Ireland with his mother.

The Tinkers were also known as the Traveling People. It was theorized that they had been displaced from the land either by Cromwell, land evictions, or from the penal times.

Whether earned or not, Danny knew they had a

reputation for fighting, drinking, stealing, and violence. They were on the absolute bottom of Ireland's socioeconomic scale, and the government's attempts to settle them in one place had never been entirely successful.

But this lone, male Tinker drove no colorful horse and cart. Instead, he pulled a ragged travel trailer behind a still more ragged car. Danny decided on impulse to take a picture. He pulled the car over, aimed and clicked as the Tinker cursed him. Danny pulled hastily back onto the road.

Beyond Keatings were more abandoned cottages. Danny took out the piece of paper on which Mrs. Slattery had written directions to the old O'Flaherty homestead. A mile or two more and Danny turned off on to a rutted road.

The O'Flaherty farm was twelve acres of rocky pasture enclosed by stone walls. The land ran halfway up the side of a bald hill, facing the sea. Danny recognized the place because of the enormous boulder that stood in the front yard of his cousin's home. Danny remembered his father mentioning the rock. The boulder was like something from Stonehenge. It dwarfed the house itself, which was a relatively new, modern bungalow, one of the homes that the government had helped farmers build in the west.

Danny felt the same surge of emotion he had felt when first arriving in Ireland. This was the land upon which his grandfather had been born. Beside the new house he saw a rotting and half-collapsed thatched-roof cottage, its stone walls crumbling. Half of the chimney had fallen over and a rusted tractor stood inert in the front yard. This, he knew, was the actual house where Daniel P. O'Flaherty had grown up. It looked like it had been abandoned for some years, although Mrs. Slattery said that Rose had moved out of the cottage into the new government-built house only five years ago.

Danny parked on the pebble drive of the new house and got out. The sky had cleared to the west and Danny could smell the sea and hear the shrieks of sea gulls.

He was nervous. He had communicated with his cousin by letter, but now that he was here, he felt a twinge of apprehension. What was he to expect?

He knocked tentatively at the door. No one came. He knocked again louder, his heart thumping. No answer.

He knocked again. "Rose? It's Danny O'Flaherty."

In the distance he could hear the screech of the sea gulls. Then he heard a long, drawn-out shriek that was not a seagull, but a shrill wail, like some animal in pain. This time he pounded louder. No reply.

She's an old woman, Danny thought. Probably a little bit deaf. "Rose," he yelled, beating on the door. "It's Danny O'Flaherty from America." No answer.

"Dammit!" Danny muttered. He had made it clear that he was coming in the morning. A small, green Morris Minor was parked beside the house. Obviously she had not gone out. Where the hell was she, he wondered.

He walked around to the back where another door led to a small yard. "Rose," he called, knocking.

Puzzled, he looked around, but there was no sign of anyone. At the side of the house was a vegetable garden. The rows of potatoes and onions had been carefully hoed and weeded. A pair of work gloves lay beside a rake and a hoe. Apparently she had been working in the garden. Perhaps she's just out for a walk, Danny concluded.

A raven croaked at him from a squat bush. Then, something sticking from behind a mound of dried turf caught his eye. He looked carefully. It was a boot. One of those rubber boots people called Wellingtons. Danny walked over to the pile of turf and looked behind it.

What he saw took his breath away. An old woman lay sprawled on the ground, her head in a puddle of fresh blood. She wore a blue house dress and the Wellingtons. Her hair was gray and her right arm was twisted up underneath her. Beside her was a *slane,* a turf spade, its blade spattered with blood.

Danny bent down for a closer look. One side of her head had been crushed by the *slane.* He reached out and turned the spade over, then looked back at his cousin. He picked up the twisted end of a hand-rolled cigarette that lay beside her. He sniffed it, and put it in his pocket.

"My God," someone gasped.

Danny looked up, startled, a look of horror on his face. It was Liam Flynn, the neighbor he had met in Larkin's Pub.

Flynn was blessing himself furiously. "May Jesus and all his holy saints have mercy on her."

Danny looked at him, dumbfounded. "She's dead," he said stupidly, as if she no longer required mercy.

"Then may God have mercy on you," said Liam Flynn.

# FOUR

GARDA KELLEY arrived soon after the startled Liam Flynn ran off, yelling for help. When Kelley pulled up in the car with Liam Flynn beside him, the garda looked belligerent.

"I knew you were a blackguard the minute I laid eyes on you," he said, stepping out of the car.

Danny stood speechless while Kelley flipped open a notebook and took a ball-point out of the top pocket of his uniform.

"What time did you get here?"

"I just arrived," Danny said.

"So you're claiming," Kelley said, looking at his watch, "that you got here about ten a.m."

"Yeah, that's about right."

"And you brought the *slane* with you, or found it here?"

"Brought it with me?" Danny asked incredulously.

"Just answer the question," said Kelley roughly, pumped up with his own importance.

"I found it here, lying beside her, with blood all over it and her head bashed in, for God's sake!"

Kelley wrote something in his book. "We'll

have it dusted for prints, of course. I want you to stop by the barracks later this afternoon so I can take your prints as well."

Kelley looked the body over carefully, making notes.

Yet Danny had the distinct impression that the garda hadn't the least idea of what he was looking for. He had probably never investigated a murder in his entire career.

For the first time, the tragedy hit Danny. This was the daughter of Danny's great-uncle, and though he had only known Rose through letters, he felt a deep sympathy. Why in the world would anyone want to kill an old woman? Then he remembered what Liam Flynn had said the night before in Larkin's: he'd said he had been trying to get Rose's farm for years.

Danny watched Flynn as he looked around the property. Sizing it up, Danny thought.

"When did you last communicate with the deceased?" asked Kelley.

"Last night. I called her just before I went in to Larkin's, about six or seven."

"Did you argue with her?"

"Argue with her?" This is absurd, Danny thought. This guy Kelley is as dumb as a truckload of bricks. He could be dangerous. "I came here to see the house where my grandfather was born, and to collect information on my family history. What would we have to argue about?''

"Sure, I wouldn't know," said Kelley.

Garda Kelley walked around the body again.

Rose O'Flaherty Noonan wore a gold band on her left hand and a jeweled wristwatch.

Whoever killed her, Danny thought, certainly didn't intend to rob her.

Danny watched as Garda Kelley turned over the hand with the wristwatch. The crystal of the watch was shattered. Apparently, when she had fallen after the blow, she had struck her watch against a rock on the ground. The hands were frozen at 9:38. The body had not yet stiffened. Kelley wrote something in his book.

"Have you asked Liam Flynn what he was doing here this morning?" Danny asked boldly.

"I have not."

Suddenly Danny thought of the Tinker he had seen on the way to his cousin's house. The Tinker had been coming from the direction of the O'Flaherty farm. He started to mention this to Garda Kelley, but then decided against it. Why should he tell this fool anything?

Danny looked at the body as Garda Kelley moved around it, taking notes. Apparently she had died from a single blow to the head. There appeared to be no sign that she had struggled with her assailant, no ripped clothes, no bruises other than the gaping wound on the back of her head. It was quite possible that she had known her murderer.

She would have known Liam Flynn, Danny was thinking, but she would not have known the Tinker. Flynn would have a motive. He had said at the pub that he wanted to marry Rose, but she had refused him. It seemed he wanted to marry their farms as much as themselves. Since their farms were adjacent, apparently Flynn was interested in combining the land of the two farms.

But what motive could the Tinker have had? It didn't seem to be robbery. When Danny spotted the Tinker, his caravan had been pulled to the side of the road. As Danny recalled, the Tinker was just getting back into the car. Perhaps he had hidden something in the pasture beside the road. Danny made a mental note to go back to the spot and see what he could find.

An ambulance pulled up with two attendants in white smocks. The attendants eased the body onto a stretcher and covered it with a white sheet. Garda Kelley gave them orders as they lifted it into the ambulance, then turned on Danny.

"What relation were you to Rose?"

"My grandfather O'Flaherty and her father were brothers."

"So, she'd be your first cousin once removed,"

Kelley said, writing something on his pad. "And what was your business with her?"

Danny considered the question carefully before answering. "I came only to learn more about the O'Flaherty family."

Kelley sniggered. "You did, did you?"

"That's right."

"Mr. O'Flaherty," Kelley said with a sigh, as if his patience were being sorely tested, "I hope you have no plans to leave the country any time soon. I'm not arresting you...yet. But you are under suspicion in the murder of Rose O'Flaherty Noonan. You will be available for further questioning when need be."

"But this is absurd, I came out here—"

"I'll get a full statement from you later. Meanwhile, I will inform all points of entry and departure in case you take a notion to cut your holiday short."

Danny couldn't believe what was happening to him.

"There's really no place for you to go, Mr. O'Flaherty," said Garda Kelley, smirking. "After all, you're on an island."

BACK AT SHANNONSIDE, Mrs. Slattery said, "You look like you've just seen a ghost," as Danny walked into the house.

Danny stood for a moment in a daze, looking at the old woman.

"Tea?" asked Mrs. Slattery.

Danny nodded, plopped in a chair in front of the turf fire, and ran his hand through his hair. When Mrs. Slattery returned with the pot of tea and a tray of scones, Danny said: "Rose is dead."

Mrs. Slattery drew her breath in sharply, put down the tea things, blessed herself, and murmured: "May the Lord have mercy on her. What happened?"

"She was murdered."

"Murdered?"

Danny poured himself a cup of tea with a shaky hand and sipped absently. "Yes."

"My God, child, when? Who?"

"It must have been about nine-thirty this morning." Danny looked around nervously and added, "I'm the chief suspect."

"What?" Mrs. Slattery shouted, spilling tea on herself.

"Liam Flynn came over just as I found her lying on the ground. She had been hit over the head with a turf spade. Flynn went running and came back with Garda Kelley. Kelley said I was not to leave the country until his investigation was complete."

"That man's an *amadán*," said Mrs. Slattery hotly. "And at the rate he works, you'll be dead yourself before his investigation is complete."

"I don't know what to do. This is just terrible. I feel so bad about Rose. But for me to be accused of being involved," Danny shuddered, "is a nightmare."

Mrs. Slattery sat upright in her chair and wagged her finger at him. "Then you need to get to the bottom of this yourself."

"Who would want to kill Rose?"

Mrs. Slattery grew misty-eyed for a moment, as if the news had finally settled over her. She dabbed at her eyes with a napkin. "Your cousin was a wonderful woman, Danny. But in a small town such as this, you have your friends and you make enemies, as well."

"Enemies who would want to kill her?"

"I'd have never imagined it," said Mrs. Slattery.

"Enemies like Liam Flynn?"

"Sure, Liam could not exactly be called an enemy," said Mrs. Slattery smiling wistfully. "He loved her in his own foolish way."

"Loved to get her farm, you mean?"

"Sure, Danny, it would have been a great match for just that reason. She with her twelve acres, milking the cows herself, bringing in the hay as best she could. And he on the other side of the ditch doing the same chores. Sure, and it would have been a fine match for that alone."

"Did he ask her to marry him?"

"Danny, he asked her to marry him every year for the past ten years, ever since her own husband died. He'd ask her every Christmas Eve and she'd turn him down. Then every New Year's Eve, he'd ask her to sell him the farm. This has been going on now for ten years. She broke the poor man's heart year after year."

"A man with a broken heart will do crazy things."

"Indeed he will."

"Like murder."

"I can't see it, Danny. Doesn't make sense. Not Liam Flynn."

"You know," Danny said, sipping his tea, "I heard the strangest wailing cry just before I found her. It sounded like some kind of monster or witch. It shrieked and shrieked like something I've never heard before."

Mrs. Slattery nodded her head knowingly. "That was the Banshee."

"The what?"

"The Banshee cries after old Irish families, like the O's and the Mac's. There's a man used to live down the road here that was killed one night. A lovely young fellow. The night he died, his brother was down to Larkin's and he went out and he heard this woman crying all along the valley. He wondered what in the world it was. He knew he could hear this woman crying, but he couldn't fathom out what was wrong. Then when he came down in the morning to First Mass, he saw this car in this place that used to be an old quarry and the gardas were around it. The car had tipped over into the quarry and his brother was in it. Killed. They said he had too much of the drink taken.''

''But what was the crying?''

''That was the Banshee. The fellow's name was McLaughlin, and the Banshee always screams before the death of an O or a Mac.''

Danny shivered from the weirdness of the tale and remembered the strange cry he'd heard before he found Rose's body. To change the subject, he brought up the Tinker. ''I saw a Tinker man coming from the direction of the farm just before I got there.''

''Sure, and what have the poor Tinkers to do with it?''

''I don't know. I was just thinking he was coming from the direction of the farm when I passed him.''

Mrs. Slattery put her cup of tea down in front of her carefully, and brushed a loose hair away from her face. She had thick, reddish fingers and the knuckles of a woman who had worked equally in the garden and the kitchen. ''Over where ye were today, now lots of people were evicted because they couldn't pay their rents or rates. They would have no place to go, so they went out on the roads, fixing pots and trading horses and such-like. They eventually became, in today's world, the Tinkers. Sure there are blackguards among them. But you've no right to think that because a man's a Tinker he's to be a suspect in every crime committed about the place.''

"Well, I just thought maybe…''

"You talk about murder and death,'' Mrs. Slattery said, her voice rising, "we've seen death here. In the time of the Famine, the churchyards in all the different places around were not big enough to bury the people, they were dying so fast. This man named McGuire gave an acre of ground out beyond your cousin's farm and any man that had a horse had to go once a week to take the bodies out to the graves. They'd be drinking this *poitin,* moonshine, homemade whiskey, and when it'd come to evening time they put the bodies up in the cart and they'd make the horses go fast. They'd have a sip of the drink taken during the day and they'd be hungry. And sure they'd often dump bodies on the ground along the way. They'd take them to that acre of ground and throw them there, and they'd shake lime on them. The priest would come along in the evening and bless the graves.'' Mrs. Slattery breathed deeply and lowered her voice. "There's twenty thousand souls buried in that acre of ground.''

"Twenty thousand?''

"Aye, Danny. You couldn't count the troubles we've seen in the west of Ireland."

The tea kettle whistled in the kitchen and Mrs. Slattery heaved herself up on her feet and shuffled off to look after it.

Danny sat ruminating, not on the deaths of the twenty thousand, but on the one death that had touched his life. Perhaps Mrs. Slattery was right. It wasn't fair to accuse the Tinker of murder just because he was a Tinker, nor Liam Flynn just because he would have liked to have had Rose's farm. But after all, Danny's life was at stake, too. He must find out who killed his cousin.

Danny thought back to the discussion in the pub the night before. Apparently there was an old feud between Brendan Grady's family and the O'Flahertys. It had something to do with politics. Brendan had said that after the Easter Rebellion, Daniel P. O'Flaherty had sided with the Free Staters, and Brendan's grandfather had died in the service of the Irish Republican Army. Was there even a remote possibility that this old feud could have something to do with Rose's death?

When Mrs. Slattery returned with yet another fresh pot of tea (how much tea do these people drink? Danny wondered), he asked her about the feud.

"You know, Brendan Grady told me last night that there was a bit of a feud between my grandfather and his grandfather. Do you know anything about that?''

"'Course I do. Brendan's grandfather was a hot-head, just like he is. Your grandfather, or so the story goes, like many Irishmen of his time, including my own father, wanted Ireland to be free of British rule. My father and your grandfather both fought with Brendan's grandfather in the old IRA. But sometime around nineteen twenty-two when the Anglo-Irish Treaty was signed, dividing Ireland into the north and south, that wasn't good enough for Brendan's grandfather. My father and your grandfather believed they had gotten a free Ireland and that was enough. So they left the IRA after a fight with Brendan's grandfather. And the IRA are fighting yet."

"Do you think Brendan's in the IRA?"

"'Twould be none of my concern if he was," said Mrs. Slattery.

"But would Brendan hold a grudge?"

"Danny, for some people the past is never forgotten. There's a story told that when de Valera himself was just a wee boy out in County Limerick, he witnessed a man being shunned by all his neighbors on the way to Mass. Why? Because the man was the descendant of an informer from the old days."

"You know, Mrs. Slattery, I think there was something Rose wanted to tell me."

"What do you mean?"

Danny took the letter from his pocket that he had received from Rose. "She says here, in nearly the last line," and Danny read aloud from the letter: "'I have some information about your grandfather that I think you would find very interesting.'"

Danny looked up at Mrs. Slattery, who seemed again to be overcome with emotion about the death of her neighbor, for tears were glistening in her eyes.

"What do you make of that?" Danny asked her.

She wiped her eyes with her napkin and gathered up the cups and saucers. "Sure, I wouldn't know. It's often I think it's best to let the dead lie in peace. Haven't they seen enough turmoil and suffering?"

"Well, maybe so," Danny said.

Danny spent the rest of the day in his room trying to piece together what little information he had about the murder. It seemed unlikely that Brendan Grady held such a grudge against the O'Flahertys that he would kill Rose. Besides, Rose's father, Sean, was never mentioned in the IRA business.

Now, the Tinker was another matter. It seemed too coincidental that the Tinker would be coming from the O'Flaherty farm so soon after the murder. If the Tinker didn't do it himself, certainly it would be useful talking to him. Danny decided to have his film developed in the morning and do his best to find the Tinker and question him.

Danny went to bed early in the evening, but slept fitfully. He woke several times in the night, dreaming that he heard the scream of the Banshee.

# FIVE

"ARE YE UP YET, Danny?" Mrs. Slattery called from downstairs. "We'll be off shortly."

Danny opened one eye and then another. He reached over to the night table where he had set his watch and looked at it. It was 7:15. Where, Danny asked himself, were they off *to?*

"The seven-thirty's not as crowded," Mrs. Slattery called up the stairs, "and Father O'Malley's sermons are shorter at First Mass than the others."

Danny groaned. He'd forgotten it was Sunday. Back in New York he made Mass infrequently, usually when some event at school made it necessary. It's not that he had turned his back on the Church. He certainly considered himself a Catholic. "Once a Catholic always a Catholic," was the way he thought about it, but he had lost much of his enthusiasm for the Church's teachings.

"Danny!" he heard Mrs. Slattery call from downstairs.

"I'm coming," he yelled, as he pulled on the best pants he'd packed.

Here in Ireland, he was quickly learning, the Church was nearly as powerful as the state, and had a strong influence on the people. Divorce and abortion were illegal and contraceptives were severely restricted. Nevertheless, there was devotion to the Church and the saints that was lacking in America. In Ireland, people were still visited by miracles. There was a shrine at Knock in Mayo where the Virgin was said to have appeared in 1879. Knock now had an international airport to accommodate the thousands of pilgrims who came each year to visit the shrine. And Danny had heard that there were sightings of the Blessed Virgin in towns all over Ireland, nearly every year. Moving statues were a phenomenon Danny had never even heard of before coming to Ireland. Statues of the Blessed Virgin were reported to move in various towns in Ireland.

He had even heard a rather sacrilegious joke the night before in Larkin's. Brendan Grady had asked Tim Mahoney had he heard that the statue of Our Blessed Mother in Kinsale had been knocked over by a car. "No," Tim Mahoney had responded innocently. Brendan Grady laughed and delivered the punch line in an exaggerated brogue. "Sure, wasn't she walking across the street when a motorist struck her." Everyone in the bar had roared, except old Liam Flynn. "No respect, no respect at all," he had grumbled into his stout.

"Danny!"

"Okay, okay."

Danny put on his best shirt, pulled a tie around his neck, squeezed his feet into his shoes and bounded down the stairs.

When Danny and Mrs. Slattery stepped into the one street that passed through the village, they did not turn in the direction of the church, but walked across the road toward Larkin's, where a knot of men stood in their Sunday best outside the pub.

"But aren't we going to the church, Mrs. Slattery?" Danny asked.

"Ah, sure the church down below's being repaired. We've been having Mass in the pub every Sunday for a fortnight."

"In the pub?" Danny asked in astonishment.

Mrs. Slattery, noting his tone, admonished him. "Do you think almighty God cares where you choose to worship him? We worshipped our God in worse places during the time of the Penal Laws."

The Penal Laws, Danny recalled, were passed in 1691. They excluded Catholics from owning land, holding office, teaching, and hearing Mass. In effect, they outlawed Roman Catholicism. Masses were held in secret anywhere a priest thought they would be safe.

Outside the pub, Danny saw most of the same people he had seen inside the night before. Seamus Larkin, Tim Mahoney, Liam Flynn, and several other weather-beaten farmers and others he did not recognize. Garda Kelley gave him a hard stare as he followed Mrs. Slattery into the pub.

As if by magic, the place had been transformed. The bar was draped with a linen altar cloth, and three banners, one with the Sacred Heart, another with a lamb with its leg around the cross, and a third with a Celtic cross. Other blankets were draped behind the bar to hide the shelves of liquor, bottles of stout, and the advertisements for Paddy's Old Irish Whiskey, Murphy's, and Guinness Stout.

There were mostly women inside, except for Danny. Across the way he saw Fidelma saying her beads. As Father O'Malley proceeded up the aisle in his vestments, flanked by two red-headed altar boys, the men who had been standing outside filed in and found seats in the back of the "church."

Father O'Malley turned and faced the congregation. "In the name of the Father, and of the Son, and of the Holy Spirit."

Father O'Malley was a short man with a thick, bullish neck and the shoulders of a boxer. Although he was probably approaching sixty, he still had a full head of black hair. His black eyebrows were bushy and grew together, dividing his high, sloped forehead from the dark pits of his eyes and his rough, flattened nose. With his coarse features, and broad brogue, he seemed well-suited to this rural parish. If not from Clare (Danny remembered someone saying he was a Kerryman), he was still one of their own.

"The intention of today's Mass," said Father O'Malley, "is for the repose of the soul of Rose O'Flaherty Noonan, who died yesterday."

"God rest her soul," murmured Mrs. Slattery, as she blessed herself.

"The grace of our Lord Jesus Christ and the love of God and the fellowship of the Holy Spirit be with you all."

"And also with you," the congregation answered.

Father O'Malley moved through Mass with efficiency and dignity. Although Danny was not the best Catholic, he still resented priests who rushed through the Mass, saying the prayers in a monotone, and reading from the missal as if more concerned about getting out to the golf course early than changing water and wine into the body and blood of Christ.

But Danny was unprepared for the sermon. Sermons in Catholic churches in America (or at least the ones Danny had heard) had fallen into a rather predictable pattern of soft-sell religion. But Father O'Malley's fire and brimstone was more like something Danny had heard from fundamentalist TV evangelists than from the pulpit of a Catholic Church.

First Father O'Malley railed against paganism.

Was Danny hearing correctly? Paganism? Yes, some goats had been sacrificed inside a stone fort in East Clare on May night. To Father O'Malley, this was evidence that paganism was still alive in Ireland, and was to be shunned and crushed with the same vehemence used by early crusaders in converting the Irish from their pagan worship. Then he railed against abortion, made all the worse because it was practiced in Catholic countries on the continent, even in Italy, the seat of the Holy Catholic Church. It would never, he roared, be tolerated in Ireland. "And now," he sighed, as if weighed down by all the sin in the world, "we have here in our own village the most heinous of crimes. Never in modern times, outside of acts of warfare, has one of our own been struck down by murder."

Danny glanced cautiously around. The murderer may be sitting somewhere in this church, he thought. Old Liam Flynn sat impassively, looking up at the priest. Tim Mahoney was looking down at his hands folded on his lap. Seamus Larkin wore the same angry snarl he wore in his pub. Of all the people he'd met so far, Danny thought, Seamus Larkin had the temperament for murder. But did he have a motive?

When Danny looked over, Garda Kelley was staring him straight in the face. Danny jumped slightly and looked back at the priest. Even Kelley, he thought, could have done it. How had he gotten to the murder scene so fast, anyway? Maybe he and Flynn planned it together. But why?

Danny realized that his mind had been wandering through the latter part of the sermon and most of the rest of Mass.

"The Mass is ended," said Father O'Malley.

Danny bowed his head and prayed for his cousin and that her murderer would be found.

"Go in peace, to love and serve the Lord," the priest concluded.

Outside, Mrs. Slattery stood in a knot of older parishioners and Danny made for where Fidelma Muldoon was standing. The day was bright and lovely. The sun was shining and the air smelled of turf smoke and the sea.

"Fidelma," he said, savoring the sound of her name on his lips.

"Danny, I..."

"Have you heard that I'm...a suspect?"

"Yes," she said, touching his arm. "In fact, Garda Kelley came around yesterday asking questions. I told him that you were with me in the graveyard at the time it supposedly happened. The Garda is crackers! He can't possibly continue to accuse you."

Danny was lightened by this strong show of loyalty. "Thanks, Fidelma," he whispered, but it seemed inadequate.

"Shall we have a look at the records after Last Mass, so?" asked Fidelma.

"Yes. I'd like that."

DANNY MET FIDELMA at the rectory after the last Mass.

"This way," she said, leading him into a small office in the back of the house. The enormous leather-bound church registry sat on a table.

"It starts in eighteen hundred," Fidelma told him, "and continues right up through the present. When did you say your grandfather was born?"

"I don't know the exact date. According to the marker out at the cemetery, his mother died in nineteen oh eight."

"If we guessed he was about forty when she died," Fidelma figured aloud, "he'd have been born in eighteen sixty-eight."

"No, that wouldn't be right. He emigrated around nineteen twenty-one. That would make him fifty-three when he left. He was younger—twenty-five or thirty."

Fidelma turned a page of the book carefully. "If he was twenty-five in nineteen twenty-one, he would have been born around eighteen ninety-six."

"That sounds more like it."

Fidelma turned the pages, running her finger down the columns of names. Danny followed her finger, but could not help noticing the graceful curve of her neck in back where the fine down met the reddish hairline. A window behind them allowed a shaft of sunlight to enter the room that illuminated the hollow on the right side where her collarbone met her neck.

"Nothing," she said, turning another page.

"How complete are the records?"

"I'm thinking they've been well-maintained these years. But there have been many times of trouble in this parish when perhaps things could not be as well taken care of as in other times."

She continued turning pages and running her forefinger down the long lists of names written in the curious script Danny remembered from letters his mother received from her parents and aunts and uncles.

Danny thought for a moment that perhaps his grandfather didn't belong to this parish.

Fidelma gave a little shriek. "Here!"

Danny's attention snapped back to the book where Fidelma held her finger beneath a name.

"Here 'tis. Your grandfather was baptized on May first, eighteen ninety-one. His mother Mary brought him to be baptized. His father is not mentioned. The baby would have been born two or three days before they brought him, so his birthday is probably April twenty-ninth or so."

"Wow!" Again Danny found a bit of wonder

in connecting with the distant past. He took the
notebook that he kept in his pocket and carefully
copied the entry from the registry. "That means he
emigrated to America when he was about thirty."

"True."

"What about his parents? My great-grandparents. Would their names be in the registry as
well?"

"Sure, they might. What was your great-
grandmother's maiden name?"

"Mrs. Slattery told me that she was a Galvin.
Mary Galvin."

"You don't know when she was born?"

"Well, the marker said she was sixty years old
when she died in nineteen oh eight."

"Let me see your pencil."

Fidelma took Danny's pencil and pad and made
some calculations. "So she would have been born
in eighteen forty-eight."

Fidelma flipped through the pages, beginning
with the year 1848. Finally, she found Mary Galvin.

"She was baptized on November twelfth, eighteen forty-eight."

Danny recorded it in his notebook, and studied
the page briefly. "So my grandfather was only seventeen years old when she died."

"That's right," said Fidelma. "She'd have been
forty-three when she gave birth to him."

"That's old."

"'Tis."

"What about my great-grandfather. Is he in there?"

"Should be. When was he born?"

"I'm not sure. His name is not on the marker. Only hers."

"That's right. Like I told you, there probably wasn't the money to add the name. I'm surprised Johnny and Micky never had the name added."

"Who?"

"Johnny and Micky Duffey."

"Who are they?"

Fidelma looked at him with surprise. "Your other cousins."

"Rose had brothers?"

"No. She was an only child. They're her cousins. They live up near Quilty. You mean you haven't been out to see them?"

"I've never even heard of them."

"Really?"

Danny was scribbling in his notebook again. He made a note to go see Rose's uncles. But for the time being he got back to the business of his great-grandfather. "Well, if my great-grandparents were about the same age, we should be able to find his name, too."

Fidelma searched the registry, beginning twenty years before 1848. She explained to Danny that often men married women much younger than themselves.

"Twenty years younger?" Danny asked.

"Sure. You see, a man wasn't considered a good match unless he was coming into the farm."

"Coming into the farm?"

"Going to inherit his parents' farm. That's why the Irish married so late. By the time the eldest son inherited his parents' farm he would often be in his forties. He couldn't get married before he owned the farm, because no woman would have him. So, by the time he had inherited the farm, he was considered a good match and he'd have the choice of marrying many young women."

"But what about his brothers and sisters? If only the eldest inherited the farm, how could the others ever get married?"

"Well, of course the girls would be looking for a match with an older farmer. And the brothers would have to emigrate. Only the eldest got the farm. There was nothing for the rest of them. If the girls were lucky they'd find a match. But if not, they'd emigrate too, like the brothers."

"That's awful. Why didn't they divide the farm so everyone could have a piece of it?"

"That's the way it was, Danny. The land was too poor. If they divided the land it wouldn't support a family. If they kept it in one piece it might just support one family."

"So the oldest got everything and the rest got nothing."

"That's how it was."

That was why Danny's grandfather had emigrated. His brother, Sean, Rose's father, must have been the eldest and inherited the farm. Daniel P. O'Flaherty had to seek his fortune in America.

They looked through most of the records, but found no baptismal entry for Daniel O'Flaherty, Danny's great-grandfather and the husband of Mary Galvin.

"Seems strange," said Danny.

But Fidelma took it in stride. "Those were difficult times. Some of the families living way out in remote areas couldn't always get in to register the births."

"Or maybe he lived in another parish."

"Perhaps."

There was a knock at the door and Father O'Malley walked in. "Are ye helping him find his roots, Fidelma?"

"Yes, Father."

The priest extended a weather-beaten hand to Danny. "I'm so sorry about Rose. I know you didn't know her well."

"Thank you, Father."

"Son, don't take our garda too seriously. He's doing the best he can with the few gifts God gave him."

"Well, he's made some strong accusations."

"He'll get to the bottom of it, eventually."

"Someone better," said Danny.

The priest indicated the registry. "Carry on. Don't let me interrupt you."

"We're finished now, Father. I'll show Danny to the door."

When the priest left, Danny pocketed his notebook. "Thanks for everything, Fidelma. You've been a great help."

"Not a bit of it."

"How about that drive to the Cliffs of Moher?"

"I'd be free tomorrow."

"Isn't Quilty up in that direction?" Danny asked.

"'Tis."

"Maybe you could show me where Johnny and Mickey Duffey live, then."

"Sure, we could stop out that way on our way to the cliffs. The poor men are bachelors, living out on that bit of land all by themselves. Sure they'd be glad for the company."

"Thanks, Fidelma."


IT WAS LATE afternoon when Danny got back to Shannonside. Mrs. Slattery wasn't home. Perhaps she'd gone to visit friends, Danny thought.

Upstairs Danny noticed that the door of his room was slightly ajar. He hesitated for a moment outside the door, thinking that perhaps Mrs. Slattery was cleaning. But no sound came from inside.

I must be getting paranoid, Danny thought.

He pushed open the door and stepped inside. One look at his suitcase told him that someone had been in his room. He had left it lying flat in front of the bed. Now it was standing up.

Danny opened the suitcase and saw that someone had been rummaging through it. Impulsively, he slapped his jacket pocket for his passport. Thank God he carried his passport and travelers checks with him. He looked around the rest of the room. Things had been moved, but nothing appeared to be missing.

Who in hell was snooping around his room? Danny wondered. Mrs. Slattery? Garda Kelley? Then he thought of the letter from Rose. He dug through the papers in the side compartment of his suitcase and sure enough, the letter was gone.

Danny sat on the edge of the bed, shaking slightly. For the first time since coming to Ireland he felt isolated and alone. He asked himself what he knew about the murder of Rose O'Flaherty Noonan. A woman of nearly seventy years, she had been killed at approximately 9:38 AM from a blow by a *slane* to the back of the head. Her husband had died ten years before. He knew that she had one daughter living somewhere in Ireland.

Clearly, whoever had broken into his room was

afraid that Danny had some information that might link him (or her) to the crime. But only the letter was missing.

Danny sat on the bed in a daze for most of the afternoon, trying to put the pieces together. When Mrs. Slattery called him to a dinner of roast mutton, boiled potatoes, and tea, he watched her carefully lest she tip her hand in some way. But the old woman chattered on about today's meeting of the Legion of Mary, of which she was president.

By the time dinner was over, Danny felt guilty for even suspecting her of going into his room.

"I'm turning in early tonight, Mrs. Slattery," Danny told her.

"You could use a good sleep, Danny. These have been trying days."

I need all the rest I can get, he thought. Because tomorrow I'm going to start asking some questions around this place.

# SIX

DANNY SPENT Monday morning reviewing the notes from his genealogical research. He also tried to match motives to the suspects he had for Rose's murder and to think of who might have broken into his room. But nothing was conclusive. Liam Flynn certainly had the motive, as well as the opportunity, since he lived next to Rose. But Danny needed more information than that to go on.

Just before noon he went over to check on his pictures at the Chemist's Shop ("drug store," Danny translated). They had promised twenty-four hour development and to Danny's surprise, the pictures were ready.

He flipped through them rapidly, interested only in the picture of the Tinker. Although it was slightly out of focus, it was still a good photo. The Tinker looked about fifty years old. But knowing the difficult lives of the Tinkers, Danny reasoned that he could be younger. His hair was black and he looked as though he had missed a few days shaving; he wore a brown suit jacket and felt hat, and he was scowling into the camera.

Danny could not tell, from the picture, what kind

of car he was driving. Nevertheless, the photo would help in finding the Tinker. Danny felt sure that he was on to something, but he didn't want to get overconfident. He reminded himself that he must pursue every possible angle.

He put the pictures into his coat pocket and walked over to Larkin's Pub. When he pushed open the door of the pub, he felt a certain chilliness from the patrons. Seamus Larkin was behind the bar, as usual, pulling a pint of stout for Tim Mahoney, who sat reading *The Irish Times*. Liam Flynn sat near the turf fire, nursing a stout. When did Flynn ever get any farming done? Danny wondered.

"Give me a pint of Harp," Danny told Seamus Larkin.

Larkin said nothing as he pulled the pint of lager for Danny and set it in front of him on the bar.

Danny handed him two pounds, picked up his pint, and pulled up a chair beside Liam Flynn. He saw Tim Mahoney look up from his paper, then bury his face behind the news again.

"Mind if I have a seat?" Danny asked, sitting down before the old man had time to reply.

Liam Flynn grunted and fiddled with his pipe.

"Mind telling me what you were doing at Rose's?"

"When?"

"You know when."

Flynn pushed the contents of his pipe with his thumb, struck a match, held it to the bowl, and sucked noisily. "I was going over to ask would she sell me her land."

"I thought you only did that on New Year's."

Liam Flynn did not seem bothered. "I've tried to talk sense into her on every day of the year."

"Why are you so anxious to own that land?"

"I knew she'd have no one to care for it once she's gone. All she has is the one daughter, and sure she'll not be coming back to Clare. I have a son living in Dublin. When I'm gone, he's promised me he'll come back and take up the farm. If he had my land and Rose's, maybe he'd make a better living than I have. But that's not likely now. Sure, Rose's daughter will probably sell it to Johnny and Mickey Duffey."

"How do you know?"

"I don't. We'll see."

"Or maybe *you'll* get it now," Danny said testily, trying to see just how far he could go.

Again, Flynn seemed unconcerned. "Perhaps. We'll see."

"Where were you before you got to Rose's place?"

"At my own house, of course."

"Is there anyone who can verify that?"

"Certainly not; I live alone."

"So you may have gotten over to Rose's before I ever came?"

"And who are you with all these questions? Sherlock Holmes?"

"Listen old man, my ass is in a bind," Danny lowered his voice. He actually liked Liam Flynn, but he had to get to the bottom of this. "I've got to find out who killed Rose."

"Sure, and why don't you leave that to the *Garda Siochana?*"

Danny ignored the question. "Where were you yesterday between about noon and five o'clock?"

"Here in the pub."

"That's right, O'Flaherty," Seamus Larkin called from behind the bar. "I'll verify that!"

"Well, someone broke into my room yesterday and rummaged around in my stuff."

Tim Mahoney put his paper down for the first time. "What's the world coming to?" he asked rhetorically, then put his face back behind the paper.

Just then the door of the pub rattled open and a man who looked even older than Liam Flynn shuffled in. His face was worn from years of exposure; he wore dark green canvas pants, muddy Wellingtons, and a wool jacket that filled the pub with a damp, acrid smell, as if a herd of sheep had entered.

"Well, if it isn't Peadar MacGreevy. How are you, sir?" said Seamus Larkin.

"Hello, Seamus," the old man croaked. "A bottle of Jameson for the master. Put it on the bill."

Larkin took a bottle of Jameson down from the shelf, wrapped it in newspaper and handed it to the old man, who shuffled carefully out of the pub.

"Who was that?" Danny asked.

"That's old Peadar MacGreevy," Tim Mahoney called from across the room. "Works out on the Pinkerton estate."

"What does he do?"

"Takes care of the sheep. He was born on the Pinkerton estate. His father worked for the Pinkerton family, and Peadar's worked for them his entire life, too."

"He must be old."

"Nearly a hundred, they say."

"I wonder if he would have known my grandfather?"

"He may have," said Tim Mahoney. "You should ask him."

"Who would want to be rummaging in your stuff?" asked Seamus Larkin, changing the subject.

"Beats me," said Danny. "Maybe it's Garda Kelley's way of investigating a murder." Danny reached into his pocket and pulled out the photograph. "Ever see this man around?" he asked, handing the photo to Liam Flynn.

Flynn made a production of getting his glasses out of his jacket pocket, adjusted them just-so on the bridge of his nose, and studied the photo carefully. "I have not," he said definitively, handing the photo back to Danny.

"What about you, Tim?" Danny asked, standing up and walking over to where Mahoney sat, the newspaper now spread out on his lap.

"Tinker," said Mahoney, as he looked at the picture.

"Ever see him before?"

"Sure, the lot of them were camped down below Kilbaha a fortnight ago. 'Twould be one of them, I'm thinking. But I don't remember this man specifically."

"Let me see," said Seamus Larkin, as he came around from behind the bar and reached for the photograph. He looked at it carefully. "I saw this man on Saturday, passing through the village pulling a caravan behind a car."

"What time?"

"I'm thinking it was around half-eight."

"Which way was he going?"

"Toward Kilbaha."

Toward the farm, Danny thought. "What kind of car was it?"

"I can't remember. What's the meaning of it?"

"I don't know," said Danny. "It's just that he passed me as I drove out to Rose's house the morning she was killed."

"What's that supposed to prove?" asked Seamus Larkin.

Danny took a sip of his Harp. "Maybe nothing." He took his glasses off and wiped them with his handkerchief. He kneaded his eyes with the tips of his fingers, replaced his glasses and took another swallow of Harp. "What about you, Tim?" Danny asked, as nonchalantly as he could. "Where were you Saturday morning between, say, nine and ten?" Danny was trying to make this as pleasant as possible.

Tim Mahoney was more than cooperative. He patiently put down his paper once again and folded his hands in his lap as if praying. "Well, believe it or not, I was not far from Rose's house."

"You were?"

"I was tramping around the back side of the Pinkerton estate. Making some notes on the ring fort back there. Measuring the circumference and the diameter, to be exact."

"Did you see anybody coming to or from Rose's house?"

"Well, no, I didn't. But then I wasn't looking for anyone either. Sure, when I get out in the fields, I kind of lose myself, if you know what I mean.

When I'm looking at the forts and suchlike, my mind is a million miles away from the present.''

"It's not right to disturb the ring forts," said Liam Flynn. "Brings bad luck."

"I suppose," Seamus Larkin snarled, "you'll want to know where I was when your cousin was killed?''

"Do we know when she was killed?" Danny asked smartly.

"Well, you said," Larkin sputtered, at a rare loss for words, "sometime between nine and ten."

Danny let it pass, but took note of Larkin's nervous manner. Yes, of all of them, Seamus Larkin seemed the most capable of bashing in someone's skull with a turf spade. "Well, where were you?''

"On my way to Kilkee. I'd to go to the hardware there to purchase some piping for the sink behind the bar.''

"Which store?"

"Harris Brothers.''

Danny made a mental note to check his alibi.

The atmosphere in the pub was tense. Danny was relieved when Brendan Grady came into the pub, greeting everyone in good spirits. In an effort to lighten the mood further, Danny pulled out his wallet. As much as he hated to part with the money, he announced. "Let's have another round for everyone, Seamus.''

"Ah, grand," cried Grady. "I'm dying with the thirst."

Tim Mahoney finished off his stout quickly in anticipation of the coming round, and Liam Flynn watched greedily as Seamus pulled three stouts and a Harp.

"The stout too heavy for you, Yank?" Seamus Larkin said derisively, in reference to Danny's preference for Harp.

"Just wanted a change," Danny said, holding his temper, knowing that his manhood was being called into question. He turned to Brendan Grady. "Where were you Saturday morning?" he asked point-blank.

"Dead to the world," he said, then caught himself and apologized quickly. "Sorry, I meant no offense. Poor Rose, God rest her soul." He recovered quickly and plunged on. "As you know, I'd had a bit too much of the drink taken Friday night. Sure, I could hardly lift my head from the pillow what with it pounding like a locomotive."

"You stayed in bed?"

"Slept 'til nearly two. Then I was back here by three for a hair of the dog that bit me. It's the only cure."

Brendan Grady was too young and too intelligent to ruin his life with drink, Danny thought.

"That's when I heard about poor Rose. I'm sorry, Danny."

"Do you live alone?" Danny asked.

"No. Me and the Da and me sister."

"Were they home Saturday?"

"No. They were off to morning Mass. Since the church is being worked on, most everyone goes to daily Mass in Kilkee."

Suddenly it occurred to Danny that at the time Rose was killed most of the villagers of Ballycara would have also been at Mass in Kilkee.

Seamus brought the pints around and set them before the men, just as Garda Kelley walked into the pub.

"Welcome, Donal," Seamus called cheerfully. "The Yank is after buying us a round. Will you join us?"

"The Yank will not be inclined to buy anyone a round after the news I have."

The mood that had been for a moment cheerful became menacing. Garda Kelley removed his hat and set it on a table. He remained standing, with his legs slightly apart and his arms crossed over his chest. "The report's back from the lab. The only fingerprints found on the murder weapon were Danny O'Flaherty's."

Danny looked up as if he had been struck. He remembered in a flash that he had knelt beside Rose, then reached out and touched the *slane*. For no apparent reason, he remembered, he had picked it up and moved it.

Having delivered his piece of evidence, Garda Kelley basked in the warm glow of power and self-importance.

But Danny was determined not to be intimidated. "Sure, I touched the *slane* after I arrived and found Rose dead," he said to everyone in the pub. "So what? Who did the *slane* belong to?"

Garda Kelley seemed taken aback. "Belong to?"

"Yeah, whose *slane* was it?"

Before Garda Kelley could reply, Liam Flynn spoke up, a note of concern in his voice. He directed his comments to Garda Kelley. "I've been meaning to report," Flynn began haltingly, "that a *slane's* been missing from the shed beside my house. I didn't notice it until this morning. Why would I notice it? I haven't cut my own turf in years." He looked around the pub nervously. "What's the use? The machines cut the turf faster than a hundred men can. I buy my turf from Pinkerton. So that old *slane's* been sitting in the shed without being moved for years now. Then this morning, I was around back looking for a rake when I noticed the *slane* missing." Flynn looked around for support. "I meant to come and tell you this morning, Donal."

"Didn't you see the *slane* at Rose's house and wonder how it got there?" Danny asked.

Garda Kelley broke in sharply. "Who's asking the questions around here?"

"The Yank's been asking plenty of them," Seamus Larkin said sourly.

"Sure and why shouldn't he?" Tim Mahoney offered, coming to Danny's defense. "He's an O'Flaherty. He has a right to know what happened to his cousin. And we've an obligation to answer his questions."

Garda Kelley poked his own chest with his forefinger. "Still, I'm the one to be asking the questions." He turned on Flynn. "Well, didn't you see the *slane* at Rose's house," he began authoritatively, then, realizing he was parroting Danny's question, he trailed off into a near whisper, "and wonder how it got there?"

"Sure, I didn't connect the two. As I've said, I haven't used that old *slane* in years. It never even occurred to me that it might have been mine."

Liam Flynn settled back into his chair as if no further explanation was needed.

Garda Kelley seemed lost; the conversation had left him momentarily befuddled. Yet he regained his authority like a loose ball that had bounced from his grasp a moment, but he was quickly able to recapture. He turned on Danny O'Flaherty. "Who owns the *slane* is of no consequence to this investigation." He shoved a crooked finger in Danny's direction. "'Twas your prints on it."

Danny said nothing. His heart beat rapidly, a wild bird in his rib cage trying to escape.

"If you'll accompany me to the barrack, Mr. O'Flaherty, I'll take your full statement." With a nearly comic display of authority, Garda Kelley snapped his hat back on his head and said with a flourish: "Good day, gentlemen."

Danny followed him sheepishly from the pub. Then he spent two hours with the man, giving a statement, which Danny signed. Again, Kelley released him on his own recognizance; he apparently had no intention of arresting him. Danny seemed to think that Garda Kelley really didn't believe he had murdered Rose, but simply enjoyed the momentary power he held over him. After all, Danny was an American, and Kelley only a small town cop on his first murder investigation.

IN THE AFTERNOON Danny drove out to the spot where he had first seen the Tinker. He edged the rented car off the road to the same spot where the Tinker had been parked. Stepping into the field beside the road, Danny looked around for anything the Tinker may have dropped or left behind. He searched the area carefully for half an hour without success. Just as he started to leave, something caught his eye. A flat stone stuck up from the ground at an odd angle. Danny walked over to it and kicked the stone over with his foot. Beneath it was a woman's leather pocketbook.

Danny looked around to see that no one was watching, then leaned over and picked up the purse. He hid it under his jacket and made for the car. In the car he opened the purse carefully and dug around inside.

He found the usual items: a tube of lipstick; a few bobby pins; an antique compact; a receipt from a dry cleaner in Kilkee—nothing much of interest. No money, no identification. If it was Rose's purse, clearly she had been robbed by the Tinker and he had hidden the evidence on his way out.

Danny eased the car back on the road and drove toward Ballycara. He was excited by the discovery, but it put him in an awkward position. Hanging onto the purse would incriminate him if anyone found it in his possession. By the same token, he didn't want to turn it over to Garda Kelley. The fellow was none too intelligent, Danny reasoned, and he would surely jump to conclusions that might be harmful to Danny's case. Better to keep the purse and find the Tinker himself. He could confide in Mrs. Slattery, but since the break-in at his room, he was no longer sure he could trust her, though he enjoyed her company immensely.

What about Fidelma? Danny wondered. He might tell her about the purse. She trusted him and could be trusted to keep a secret until he was able to find the Tinker himself. After all, how difficult could it be to find someone who drove around pulling a trailer behind a car and camping in fields?

Danny hid the purse beneath the front seat of the car and parked in front of Shannonside. Inside, Mrs. Slattery rocked in her chair in front of the turf fire, watching TV. Danny told her about his confrontation with Garda Kelley and his signed statement.

"Sure, it's not much of a holiday for ye," was all Mrs. Slattery had to say on the subject.

Danny had to agree with her. It wasn't turning out to be much of a holiday.

to find the Packet himself. After all, how difficult
could it be to find someone who drove around until
in a yellow Packet

# SEVEN

"SOMEONE'S LYING," Danny said bitterly.

He had picked up Fidelma Muldoon at the rectory at five o'clock. She was dressed in a blue cotton dress, straw hat with a blue band, and she had tied her hair back in a ponytail.

He related the conversation he had that morning at the pub with Flynn, Larkin, and Mahoney. "If Liam Flynn did use his own *slane* to kill her, certainly he wouldn't leave it there. I think someone's trying to frame the old man."

"Could be. But who?" asked Fidelma.

The road curled ahead of them through bare, green fields. The land looked too poor to support the few sheep and cattle they passed. Neat houses stood behind stone walls, but they only occasionally passed any people—farmers raking hay or pouring feed into troughs for their cattle. The land was an intense green such as Danny had never seen before, and its desolate, wild emptiness gave the landscape a mystical beauty. "I don't know, Fidelma. Seamus Larkin is certainly a disagreeable one. But what motive would he have for killing Rose?"

"None a-tall," said Fidelma. "Seamus doesn't like a single soul in the village. If he killed everyone he hated, sure no one would be safe in Ballycara."

Danny laughed. "Then there's Brendan Grady with his IRA connections."

"Ach," Fidelma waved her hand in a gesture of dismissal. "You've been reading too much of that Tom Clancy fellow."

"Well, Mrs. Slattery said people still hold old grudges."

"Sure, they do. But Brendan Grady's as harmless as a wee lamb."

"What about Tim Mahoney? Even Tim was out in that direction the day of the killing."

"Sure, you'll have the whole village responsible at the rate you're going!"

"Well, who then?" Danny shouted angrily.

Fidelma looked up, startled by the sudden violence in his voice. But far from intimidating her, it only sparked her own Gaelic temper. "Why don't you leave it to the garda? Sure, you're just a blow-in yourself."

"A what?"

"A blow-in. A stranger," she shouted, then settled back in her seat with a pout.

"You know," Danny said quietly, "it seems Father O'Malley was trying to rush us off yesterday from reading the record."

Fidelma sighed, "Oh, for the love of God! He just happened to pop in. I suppose he's a suspect as well?"

"I don't know; he just seemed to be rushing us if you ask me."

"That's cod! Why would he do that?"

"Maybe there is something in the record he didn't want me to find."

"For example?"

"I don't know."

Fidelma reached over and touched his arm. "Aren't you getting a bit carried away with yourself, Danny?"

Danny looked out the window. Maybe he *was* getting carried away. But he was supposed to fly home in a week. There was no telling now how long he'd be here while Garda Kelley stumbled around trying to find Rose's killer.

They passed through Furroor, and Kilfearagh. As they approached Kilkee, Danny suggested that they stop in at Harris Brothers.

"Seamus Larkin told me that at the time of the murder he was in Harris Brothers buying piping for his sink at the pub."

"Don't you believe him?"

"I didn't say I didn't believe him," Danny said defensively. "I just want to check it out."

On the outskirts of Kilkee, Danny turned where Fidelma directed. The seaside resort of Kilkee was

a popular spot for Irish and English tourists who
wanted sun, its wide sandy beach, and the cliff
views just outside of town. Danny drove up a narrow lane lined with shops and soon came to the
Harris Brothers store. He parked in front. Fidelma
waited in the car while he went inside.

"Excuse me," Danny said to the elderly clerk
behind the counter, "but I'm a friend of Seamus
Larkin."

"Ah, Seamus," the clerk's face brightened.
"Sure, I haven't seen him in ages."

"Do you work here all the time?"

"You're an American, aren't you?" the clerk
asked him.

"Well, yes. I..."

"Sure, it's not just the accent, but that direct
manner. Where are you from?"

"New York," Danny answered, feeling as
though he had lost control of the conversation.

"I'm Declan Harris," the man said offering his
hand. "My brother James is dead now. I'm the
*only* employee here."

"Was Seamus Larkin in here last Saturday?"

"No. I haven't seen Seamus in a year, or more."

Danny turned and walked toward the door. As
he turned the handle to let himself out, Declan Harris called out, "How can I help you, sir?"

Danny opened the door and stepped out before

calling back over his shoulder, "You already have."

"Well?" Fidelma asked as he slammed the car door and pulled back onto the road.

"Larkin is lying."

"You mean he didn't go to Harris Brothers on Saturday?"

"Not a bit of it," Danny said, smiling at the way he was picking up the local speech. He recounted his conversation with the clerk.

"Maybe Declan Harris is lying," said Fidelma.

"I don't think so. Why would he?"

They fell silent for a time as Danny awkwardly shifted gears with his left hand. He still found it difficult driving on the left side of the road.

So Larkin was lying about where he was at the time of the murder. This was the best break he'd had since finding the purse under the rock. But it was still a further complication. Were Larkin and the Tinker somehow in cahoots? Danny hadn't mentioned finding the purse to Fidelma. He wondered whether he should tell her. Possession of the purse would be incriminating enough to make Garda Kelley do something drastic if he found out.

"Fidelma…" Danny began.

"Yes?"

Danny started to tell her about the purse, but then changed his mind. Better wait until he had more evidence. "Nothing."

"You're a queer one," she said.

They passed through Bealaha and Doonbeg where, Fidelma explained, there were many pubs where traditional Irish music was played.

But Danny had other things on his mind. "Maybe it was Larkin who broke into my room," he said.

Fidelma laughed. "Sure, it's hard to imagine old Seamus Larkin sneaking around poking into your things."

Beyond Doonbeg at Creegh they turned onto T-69 and drove north toward Quilty. The land was green, but desolate.

"Shall we go up to the cliffs first or stop off and see Johnny and Mickey?" Danny asked.

"Why don't we go up to the cliffs for a bit, then go and see the twins on our way back."

"They're twins?" Danny asked, surprised.

"Yes. Didn't you know that?"

"No. How old are they?"

"Sure, they must be in their eighties."

Danny downshifted as they wound their way up low hills, and through pastures of green grasses littered with boulders. Danny asked about the black spots beside the road; Fidelma explained that a black spot marked the place where someone had been killed in an auto accident. Danny smiled at the road sign: NO OVERTAKING.

At Quilty, the road hugged the rocky seashore

and Fidelma pointed out Mutton Island, barely visible offshore. Spanish Point, Fidelma explained, was named for the wreck of a ship from the Spanish Armada. The survivors of the wreck were executed by the Sheriff of Clare on orders of the Governor of Connacht. A series of mounds near the shore marked their graves.

The road more or less followed the coast, affording spectacular vistas of the Atlantic through Lahinch, with its sandy beaches and golf course, and Liscannor, a fishing village where trawlers and fishing boats were anchored. They were in the area of the Burren, a lunar landscape of bald limestone where Arctic and Mediterranean plants grew side-by-side.

Soon, the road rose dramatically. To the left, sheer cliffs dropped into the Atlantic hundreds of feet below. Danny drove to the car park; he and Fidelma got out to walk up to O'Brien's Tower at the summit of the cliffs.

''Beautiful,'' he murmured, as they climbed along the rocky trail. A sharp wind blew in from the sea, carrying with it the cries of hundreds of sea birds that nested in the sheer rock face of the cliffs.

The Cliffs of Moher are a five mile stretch of cliffs that are as high as 700 feet at their highest point. Here, Danny thought, looking cautiously over the side, it is as if Europe ended abruptly, a flat table dropping off sharply to the roiling sea that swirled and churned on the rocks below.

"There's the Aran Islands," Fidelma said, pointing out to sea.

Danny could barely make out the offshore islands that he had first seen from the airplane on his arrival in Ireland.

Gusts of wind swept the flat area where they stood high above the sea; Danny and Fidelma struggled slightly to stand. Fidelma had pulled the straw hat from her head and the Atlantic winds swept her red hair back from her face. Danny reached out to steady himself, and Fidelma took his hand as they walked along the cliffs, watching the gulls tack out to sea against the strong currents of air.

"Fidelma..." Danny said. He stopped and looked her in the eyes.

She nibbled her bottom lip nervously and looked up at him, her eyes twinkling. "Yes?"

"What if Larkin and the Tinker somehow planned Rose's murder together?"

"Oh, for God's sake," she said, exasperated. She dropped his hand and turned from him to face the ocean. "Can't you get your mind off that just for the afternoon?"

"No," Danny said, offended. "No, I can't."

Fidelma heaved a sigh and looked at Danny, shaking her head slightly. "I could easily imagine

Seamus Larkin killing someone. But it would have to be for a good reason. Larkin wouldn't do anything unless he could make a pound or two doing it. But it seems unlikely that he would have robbed your cousin. If robbery was a motive, then your man the Tinker's a more likely candidate, I'm thinking.''

Danny thought of the purse. He wanted to share this evidence with Fidelma, but was still reluctant. ''Yeah, the Tinker would be the most likely to rob her. But he wouldn't go over to Liam Flynn's house, borrow his *slane,* threaten Rose with it, knock her over the head, leave the *slane* there and run. It doesn't make sense.''

''None of it makes sense if you ask me.''

''By the same token, why is Larkin lying about where he was at the time of the murder?''

''Sure, I've no more insight into the affair than you have yourself.''

''What about Pinkerton?''

Fidelma seemed surprised by the question. ''Ah, yes, there's always Pinkerton, isn't there?''

''What do you mean by that?''

''Sure, you've accused every villager in Ballycara who wasn't at Mass in Kilkee that morning; it's only natural you'd turn on Pinkerton.''

''Well,'' Danny said defensively, ''his land borders Rose's, too. Maybe he also wanted to get the farm.''

Fidelma laughed openly, shaking her head. "Danny O'Flaherty, you must think those twelve acres of your cousin's are Phoenix Park. Sure, they're poor as stones. Nobody wants Rose's land. You've seen too many Westerns."

Danny bristled from the insult. In fact, he found Fidelma's attitude generally uncooperative, and she was making him out to be a fool. By God, he would find out who killed Rose, and he'd show Fidelma Muldoon just who the fool was.

As they left the cliffs, a misty drizzle began to make driving difficult. Danny flipped on the wipers and they drove in silence through the rain. The lack of visibility made it all the more harrowing since the image of the 700-foot sheer drop to the sea was clearly in Danny's mind.

Outside of Quilty, they turned onto a rutted secondary road. The tires of the car flung up chunks of stone that banged on the floor beneath them. The road was narrow, with low walls of stone (ditches, Fidelma called them) on both sides. They scraped across a small creek bed, up a hill and down. The left front wheel went into a hole and smacked the frame of the car down on a protruding rock.

"Are you sure this is the way?" Danny asked nervously.

"'Tis."

Then the back wheel fell into the same hole and a rock crashed up against the gas tank. Danny cringed. The rain had slackened off slightly. A small creek gurgled softly over the roadway. Danny drove down into the shallow creek and the car groaned as it scrambled up the other side.

Straight ahead, a small whitewashed cottage stood alone, surrounded by fields of hay. The cottage was made of stones with a chimney at each end, from which smoke curled. The thatch roof was in good repair; ropes hooked beneath the eaves kept the thatch from blowing away. A flock of sheep huddled together at one end of the cottage to escape the wind, and Danny heard the lowing of cows coming from somewhere behind the house. The air smelled of wet wool, turf smoke, and manure...an earthy, not entirely unpleasant smell.

Danny switched off the car and a scraggly dog came out barking from behind the house, scattering the sheep as it made its way toward the car.

"Well," said Fidelma, "shall we go in?"

Danny nodded.

# EIGHT

THE DOOR of the cottage opened, scaring up two hens that crouched against the rain in the doorway. An elderly man with a bright, round face stuck his head out of the top half of the double doors. He was dressed in a worn, wool cardigan pulled over a brown sweater, and a tweed cap that had seen better days. When he opened the bottom half of the door and stepped out, Danny saw that his pants were a lusterless corduroy with a patch over the right knee.

"That's Johnny Duffey. Sure, he probably won't know me a-tall. It's been so long since I've been out here."

Fidelma opened the car door and stepped out. She held her hat on her head against the drizzle and ran toward the cottage. Danny jumped out after her.

"Fidelma!" Johnny Duffey shouted with surprise.

Fidelma turned to Danny. "Sure, he does remember me."

Johnny Duffey opened the door wider and let them in. He was a grizzled, bearish man with a wide, reddish face covered with stubble, and when he took off his cap, Danny noticed that his brown hair was thinning on top. Johnny looked around apologetically. "Ah, the place is a shipwreck," he said.

"That's all right," said Fidelma. Then, turning to Danny she added, "There's only the two of them, you know."

Danny looked around in wonder. The cottage reminded him of pictures he had seen of the Ireland of his grandfather's time. It had a cold, stone floor and a great open hearth. The fireplace was recessed, with a long oak mantle above it. A turf fire flickered in the fireplace. On the mantle, amid various bottles, cans, candles, and other odds and ends, stood a picture of an early 20th century Pope. Danny wasn't sure which one. In the fireplace was a metal contraption from which hung a pot of boiling stew. The room was damp and cold despite the blaze in the fireplace.

"Johnny," Fidelma said, "this is Danny O'Flaherty from America. His grandfather was Daniel P. O'Flaherty from down in Ballycara."

"Ah, sure. Where's your red hair, lad? You don't favor the O'Flahertys." Johnny Duffey's brogue was thicker than any Danny had heard so far in Ireland, and his speech was a mixture of Irish Gaelic and English.

Danny ran a hand through his black curls. "My grandfather's hair was dark."

"Sure, 'tis true," said Johnny. He gave Danny's hand a bone-shattering squeeze and pulled two more chairs up to the fire. "Sit down there," he said, pointing to the chair. "I suppose you've come over for Rose's funeral?"

"Well, not exactly. I was here the day she was killed."

Johnny Duffey shook his head. "A tragedy, a terrible, terrible tragedy. *Cá fhad a bheidh tú? ag fanacht?*"

Fidelma answered in English. "He'll be leaving in a week or so."

All three of them silently watched the flames lick the bricks of turf. Johnny Duffey got up and rummaged around in a cabinet of canned food and came up with a bottle of Paddy's Old Irish Whiskey. *"Ar mhaith libh deoch?"*

"What did he say?" asked Danny.

"Will you have something to drink," Fidelma translated.

Johnny switched to English. "Sure, I've only a bit of whiskey to offer ye."

"That's fine," Danny said.

Johnny found two tumblers and a tea cup. He poured generous shots for Danny and Fidelma in the tumblers and a shot for himself into the tea cup.

"Where's Mickey?" asked Fidelma.

"Sure, he's down below in the hay barn. He'll be up shortly. We're always working, you know."

Again, Danny struggled to follow the conversation. Compared to Fidelma's accented, yet clear speech, Johnny Duffey sounded like he was speaking a foreign language even when he spoke English.

"*Sláinte,*" said Johnny, raising his cup, and knocked off the whiskey in a gulp.

The dog came over from across the room and curled up in front of the fire at Johnny's feet.

"Now," said Fidelma, "what relation would you be to Danny, here?"

Johnny looked heavenward, as if adding up columns of figures in his head. "This boy's grandfather, Daniel P. O'Flaherty, and my mother were brother and sister."

"Really!" Danny exclaimed. "But I thought he only had one brother, Sean, Rose's father."

"Not a bit of it. There was my mother Maureen, God rest her soul, my uncle Sean, and your grandfather, Daniel. My mother married Dermott Duffey. This was the Duffey homestead here. When my parents died, Mickey and I took up the farm." He looked around him. "Sure, we haven't gone far. My father and my grandfather were both born here."

"Your mother was my great-aunt," said Danny.

"That's right. So you'd be my first cousin once

removed. In fact, I have some of the Mass cards from your family.''

Johnny got up again and rummaged in the cabinet until he found what he was looking for. He handed the holy card to Danny. It was tattered and moldy from the damp climate, and Danny held it gingerly. On the front of it was a picture of a small child picking flowers at the edge of a sharp cliff. Behind him floated an angel with wings and a halo who held her hand above the child's head. Under it was the caption: "Blessed are the dead who die in the Lord. Let them rest from their labors, for their works follow them." (Apoc. 14:13).

Danny turned the card over and read:

*Jesus Have Mercy On The Soul Of*
*Daniel P. O'Flaherty*
*Who Passed Away*

*September 6, 1960*

*O Gentlest Heart of Jesus ever present in the Blessed Sacrament, ever consumed with burning love for the poor captive souls in Purgatory, have mercy on the soul of thy departed servant. Be not severe in Thy judgment, but let some drops of Thy precious blood fall upon the devouring flames, and do Thou, O merciful Savior, send Thy angels to conduct*

*Thy departed servant to a place of refreshment, light and peace. Amen.*

Danny looked up from the card. "That's my grandfather. Where did you get this?"

"Sure, your mother sent it. We'd always hear from her when one of the family passed on. She was great for corresponding. 'Tis funny that we never heard from your da or your granda a-tall. But your mother, who wasn't even an O'Flaherty, kept in contact."

Danny looked down at the card again. At the bottom was an additional prayer by St. Ambrose: "We have loved him dearly during life; let us not abandon him until we have conducted him by our prayers into the house of the Lord."

When Danny looked up from the card his eyes were filled with tears. "Did you get a Mass card when Mother died?" he managed to ask.

"No."

Of course not, Danny thought sadly. There was no one to send one. Dad wouldn't have sent it. Only Mom cared about the people back here.

"Your mother's people were from Mayo, weren't they?" Johnny asked.

"Yeah."

"Will you be going up to see them?"

"Not this time," said Danny.

Danny took his notebook from his jacket pocket

and scribbled a few notes. Just then Mickey Duffey came in, kicking mud off his boots against the door frame.

"*Sé seo mo dheartháir é,*" Johnny said. Then in English, "Look who's here. Isn't it wee Fidelma Muldoon and Danny O'Flaherty from the States."

Although they were twins, Mickey looked older than his brother. He was thinner and more stooped and his hair had gone almost completely gray.

"God bless ye," he said to them in the traditional greeting.

Mickey pulled a crate over to the semicircle of chairs and sat down. When Johnny offered him a shot, he waved it away.

"I'm so sorry about Rose," Danny said awkwardly.

"A tragedy," Mickey said, in the exact words of his brother. "A terrible, terrible tragedy."

"Sure, what's the world coming to?" murmured Fidelma.

"Who was the oldest in my grandfather's family?" asked Danny, his pen poised above his notebook.

"Sure, your grandfather, Daniel, was the oldest. Then came Sean. Our mother was the youngest."

"What year was your mother born?"

Johnny looked at the ceiling and scratched his head in concentration. "Must have been about eighteen ninety-four."

"And Sean?"

"Eighteen ninety-eight. Sure, weren't they born one right after another."

Danny wrote the information into his notebook. "What I can't figure out," he said, "is why grandfather emigrated. Wasn't the oldest supposed to take up the farm? Instead, Sean took the farm."

Johnny and Mickey looked at each other briefly. "Sure, I wouldn't know," said Mickey. "Times were hard then. Your grandfather probably wanted more opportunity than those twelve acres were going to afford him."

"What about now?" asked Danny. "What will happen to the O'Flaherty homestead?"

Johnny looked at his brother again. Mickey got up and rummaged around in the cabinet and came back with a folded document. "Sure, wasn't the solicitor here yesterday. Here's the copy of Rose's last will and testament."

Mickey handed the document to Danny. Danny scanned quickly through the legalities and got to the heart of the matter. The few assets she had in the form of bank accounts, a few stocks, the house and two acres, were left to her only daughter, Mona Noonan, of Dublin. Ten acres, the farm equipment, and the livestock were left to Johnny and Mickey.

Danny nodded and looked up. "Do you intend to farm the land?"

Both brothers spoke at once. "We don't know." Then Johnny took over. "It came as a surprise to us."

Danny hated to probe, but it did seem odd. "Why do you think she did it this way? Why didn't she leave it all to her daughter?"

"Sure, 'tis queer," said Johnny.

Mickey answered sharply. "'Tis not queer. That daughter of hers wouldn't give a damn about the land. Sure, she'll sell that house and two acres and be on the next train back to Dublin before poor Rose is cold in her grave."

"Maybe she'll sell it to Liam Flynn," Danny said, testing.

"Ah, Flynn," said Johnny. "Sure, he'd have no use for the house. But oh, did he want that land. He's greedy, that man."

Danny fell silent for a bit. Something seemed fishy about the whole thing. Maybe it did make sense to let Johnny and Mickey farm the land. But they were old men themselves, and they had no one to leave it to when they were gone. Maybe they'd farm it for as long as they lived and then leave it to Rose's daughter when they died.

"I suppose you could always sell it to Flynn if you needed to," Danny said, trying to gauge their reaction.

Mickey raised his voice in anger. "I'd not sell that land to Liam Flynn if me life depended on it."

"Why not?"

"Sure, he's spent ten years hounding poor Rose about the land. I'd not be surprised if he killed her himself 'cause she wouldn't sell to him," shouted Mickey.

It was the first time, Danny noted, that anyone besides Garda Kelley had expressed an opinion on who might have killed Rose.

"You really think so?"

Johnny tried to calm his brother. "Sure, he's just talking. Liam Flynn'd be too afraid of spending eternity in hell to do something like that."

Fidelma giggled. "You've a point there."

But Danny wanted to hear more from Mickey. "Did you know," he asked, "that the *slane* used to kill her belonged to Liam Flynn?"

"Sure, the solicitor told us yesterday," said Mickey. "I'm sure Flynn did it, too. I tell you that man's greedy."

"If he did kill her," said Danny, "it didn't do him any good. So why would he do it at all?"

"I'm thinking he went over there to ask her to sell the farm. When she wouldn't, he lost his temper, went and got his *slane,* and broke her poor head open," said Mickey.

"Ach, Mickey," said Johnny with disgust. "You're letting your imagination run away with itself."

Something about Mickey's conviction seemed

false to Danny, and Johnny's protests seemed staged. Maybe Mickey was just trying to shift the blame to Liam Flynn in order to take the heat off himself, or someone else. After all, he and his brother were the ones who'd benefited from the murder; they were the ones who had inherited the land.

Johnny Duffey poured another shot of whiskey for himself and Danny. Fidelma and Mickey declined. Johnny's hand seemed to shake slightly as he held out the bottle. Was he nervous about something? Danny wondered.

"You know," Danny said. "We went through the church records in Ballycara and found my grandfather's baptismal record." Danny took out his notebook and flipped back several pages. "He was baptized," he read, "on May first, eighteen ninety-one."

"That'd make sense," said Mickey. "He was about three years older than my mother."

"And his mother," said Danny, referring to his notes, "was baptized on November twelfth, eighteen forty-eight."

"She was a Galvin, I'm thinking," said Johnny.

"That's right. But what seems strange," Danny said, looking up from his notes, "is that there's no mention of his father, my great-grandfather, in the baptismal record."

Johnny and Mickey said nothing.

Fidelma, who had sat quietly for some time, spoke up. "I told you yesterday, Danny, those were difficult times. People didn't always get in to church."

"That's right," said Mickey hastily. "Times were hard then. Sure, some never got around to registering births, and I'm sure some never got in to have the children baptized a-tall."

"I suppose not," said Danny.

Johnny poured another shot of whiskey into Danny's glass and another shot for himself. Danny was enjoying the whiskey, and the company, and wished for just a moment he could get his mind off the murder. These two old fellows were the genuine article.

"Did you ever hear of the Banshee?" Danny asked impulsively.

Fidelma gave a short laugh but Mickey spoke up. "Sure, I heard the Banshee meself one time."

"Oh, ho," cried Johnny, "this should be a good one."

"I did, I did," insisted Mickey. "Definitely, I did. 'Twas the night of Uncle Sean's wake. I was helping Rose lay him out. We'd to put all the different frills and everything else you had to put on the deceased. We'd to put three folds overhead and two folds underneath in honor of the five moons." Mickey Duffey's voice had changed and his eyes sparkled eerily. "And it was as bright ... the moon was bright that night. And we heard this loud crying and screaming like someone was being murdered all the while we were laying him out. And Rose asked, 'What's that?' ''Tis a fox,' said I. ''Tis not!' ''Tis,' said I, 'that's a fox.' And I was shivering now, but I couldn't let Rose know because the two of us would go to pieces and there'd be no one to get ready for the wake.''

Danny took a sip of his whiskey and shivered a bit himself. He pulled his coat tighter around him.

''Well, then we went out into the kitchen and when I closed the door after me I said, 'Rose, would you make tea quick?' I said, 'both of us can say we've heard the Banshee.' And she said, 'Didn't I tell you it was? I knew I was afraid.' And I said, 'but if I told you, none of us would have been able to do anything.''' Mickey Duffey wiped his brow. ''I tell you the sweat ran down me.''

Fidelma spoke up. ''Now, come on, Mickey. Do you expect us to believe that?''

Mickey held up his hand. ''As Christ is my Lord and Savior, I swear on my dear mother's grave that I heard the Banshee that night.''

Danny's hand trembled slightly as he held his glass out for another shot of whiskey. He wished he'd never asked about the Banshee.

The afternoon passed quickly with more whiskey and more stories. Johnny Duffey added a few more pieces of mutton to the pot that was sim-

mering in the fireplace and everyone had a bowl
of the stew. Danny took copious notes on family
history. The brothers even had an old photograph
showing Danny's grandfather as a child with his
brother and sister.

"I'm thinking we'd want to be going soon,"
said Fidelma, after Johnny Duffey had miraculously found another bottle of whiskey down in the
hay barn. Johnny had become increasingly difficult
to understand. Not only was his speech slurred, but
as the night wore on he spoke less and less English.

*"An ndéanfaidh tú? rince liom?"* he asked Fidelma.

She burst into giggles.

"What did he say?" asked Danny.

"He wants to know if I want to dance. I think
it's time we move along, Danny."

But Danny didn't want to go anywhere. He
couldn't remember being happier in his entire life.
These two cousins of his, living out in the far west
of Ireland, had a life that he envied. At least, under
the influence of numerous glasses of Paddy, it
looked pretty good. But Fidelma was insistent.

"C'mon, Danny Boy. Father O'Malley will be
wondering what happened to me."

"Ah, tell the priest to piss off," said Johnny
Duffey, who was well in his cups.

One thing Danny couldn't figure out was how
so many of the Irish could be religious, with pic-

tures of the saints and popes all over the place, yet they still seemed to dislike priests.

"Hold on, Fidelma," Danny said. But when he saw her give him an angry look, he knew it was time to go.

Danny was sorry to bid Mickey and Johnny farewell. He gave them each a warm handshake and stumbled after Fidelma out of the cottage.

Although it was almost ten-thirty, the sun had not yet gone down. The sky was salmon-colored in the west. The thatch of the cabin's roof had turned golden in the dying light and the bleating of sheep was an overture to the symphony of stars that played in the dusk.

Fidelma got behind the wheel of the car and demanded the keys from Danny.

"'Twas a grand night," Danny said in his fake brogue.

"Indeed, it was," said Fidelma.

Johnny and Mickey Duffey waved good-bye from the doorway, and the dog barked in the side yard as night came on gently as a lamb.

"*Oíche mhaith*," the brothers called. "Good-night!"

Danny reached over and attempted to put his arm around Fidelma's shoulder. "But the night's still young," he said.

Fidelma laughed good-naturedly, but brushed

his hand away. ''Not for this lass,'' she said with finality.

She backed the car out of the yard and swung it around.

''Thanks for everything, Fidelma,'' Danny said.

'''Tis nothing.''

Danny slept all the way back to Ballycara.

# NINE

THERE WAS A LETTER waiting for Danny when he came downstairs the next morning for breakfast. Mrs. Slattery handed it to him in the parlor.

"This came for you yesterday," she said, eyeing him with open curiosity.

Mrs. Slattery looked disappointed when Danny slipped the letter into his coat pocket and sat down to breakfast.

"Aren't you going to see who it's from?" she asked.

"Later," Danny said, as he brought his tea cup to his lips. Despite the bout of drinking at Johnny and Mickey Duffey's, he was feeling chipper.

Mrs. Slattery went into the kitchen and returned with the usual plate of fried eggs, rashers, *drisheen,* fried tomatoes, and brown bread.

Danny ate ravenously. Without a doubt, he concluded, breakfast was the high point of Ireland's culinary day, despite the blood pudding. He took another cup of tea and said to Mrs. Slattery, "I'm off to Ennis today."

"Oh?"

"Thought I'd go over to the courthouse and see

what I could dig up about my grandfather in the Office of Births, Deaths, and Marriages.''

"Good idea. Sure, they'd have the complete record there, I'm thinking.''

Danny took another piece of brown bread. "I remember my Aunt Annie used to make this stuff,'' he said. "It's great stuff.''

"So how are Johnny and Mickey making it?''

"Oh, they're grand. Great folks.''

"That they are.''

After breakfast, Danny went upstairs to his room to open his mail. Although there was no return address, the letter was postmarked Dublin. Danny ripped open the envelope. Inside was a handwritten note on cream-colored paper.

Mr. O'Flaherty:
I will be staying at the Old Ground Hotel in Ennis while my mother's affairs are settled. Could you ring me up or stop by? I have a few matters I'd like to discuss with you.
                                                        Mona Noonan

Well, thought Danny, that's interesting. I wonder what she wants to see me about? Was she too good to stay in Ballycara while her mother's affairs were straightened out? Danny pocketed the letter, put a few things in a bag for the road, and closed the door behind him.

He drove through Kilrush and picked up N-68 to Ennis, retracing the route he had taken when he first arrived in Ballycara.

The day was overcast and humid. In Ennis, Danny drove up busy O'Connell street toward the statue of Daniel O'Connell. He crisscrossed several narrow streets, then crossed the river Fergus and drove toward the courthouse.

He found a parking spot on a side street and walked the short distance to the courthouse. After several inquiries, he found his way downstairs to the Office of Birth, Deaths, and Marriages. An attractive woman behind a small window dealt with the long line of people waiting their turns. Most needed death certificates, or birth certificates for passports, or some other official business. Danny felt foolish waiting in line for the birth certificate of someone who had been born in the previous century.

People seemed generally unconcerned with the long wait. They chatted, smoked cigarettes, and exchanged gossip.

"Digging up your roots, are ye?" an elderly woman asked him, obviously realizing he was an American.

How could they tell? Danny wondered. Was it his clothes, the way his hair was cut? The way he smelled?

"Yes," he answered, "digging up my roots."

"Ah, sure the whole generation of them is coming back now to find their own. They come from Australia, America, England, South Africa, even South America, all looking for their Irish roots."

Danny hadn't really thought of all the other places to which Irish people had emigrated. For some reason he imagined them only going to America.

"Sure, the Irish went to the four corners of the earth during the Famine times," the woman lectured.

"That so?"

"Now all their children are coming back to find their roots," she added.

When Danny got to the window, the young woman behind the counter smiled at him and asked how she could help.

"I'd like to get a registered copy of my grandfather's birth certificate...if that's possible."

She handed him a pencil and a scrap of paper. "Would you write the name and year of birth, please."

Danny wrote: "Daniel P. O'Flaherty, 1891" on the piece of paper and handed it back. She looked at it for a moment then said, "I'll see what I can find."

She turned to a row of shelves that held enormous, leather-bound registries. She found the registry for the year 1891 and with some difficulty laid it out on a wooden table in the back of the office.

Danny felt a little embarrassed as she leisurely flipped through the registry. At least fifteen people were waiting behind him. He turned to a man and woman with two small children, who waited patiently. "I'm sorry to take up your time, I know you have more important..."

"Not a bit of it," they protested.

Several other people in line spoke up. "We're in no hurry."

The clerk was certainly in no hurry. She searched through one registry, returned it to its shelf, and took down another.

"I didn't realize it would take this long," he said to the family behind him, but they waved it off as if it were nothing.

"Are you sure he was born in eighteen ninety-one?" the woman asked.

"Well, not exactly," Danny said apologetically. "I know he was baptized in eighteen ninety-one."

She replaced the registry she had been looking through and brought another one down onto the table. Ten minutes later she said, "Here 'tis."

"You found it?"

By now everyone in line seemed involved, and someone gave an audible sigh of relief. The woman behind the counter took out a fountain pen, and an official birth certificate form, on which she copied the information from the registry:

> *Daniel P. O'Flaherty*
> *Born: July 16, 1890*

After stamping the official seal of the Republic of Ireland on it, certifying that it was a registered copy of the official registry, she handed it to Danny, who paid the seven-pound fee.

Outside, Danny sat on the steps of the courthouse and looked over the document. He was still amazed that after all these years one could go into a courthouse and get a record of a birth that had taken place over one hundred years before.

Danny decided to leave his car where it was parked and walk to the Old Ground Hotel, so he could see a bit more of the town. Again he crossed the River Fergus and walked to O'Connell Square, where the statue of Daniel O'Connell stood surveying the main thoroughfare of Ennis. It was a pleasant town, with numerous shops opening on to the busy main street, and a myriad of cobblestone streets leading off in various directions.

He stopped at a small shop and had a bowl of clam chowder, a sandwich, and a cup of tea. He studied the birth record as he ate.

It seemed odd that his grandfather had been baptized ten months after he was born, Danny mused.

Normally, a Catholic child was baptized immediately to ensure his entrance into heaven. Danny recalled a story Mrs. Slattery had told him about places where unbaptized babies were buried; nearly every community had a small plot of land where unbaptized babies were buried, because it was forbidden for them to be buried in the church cemetery. What Catholic parents of the 19th century would risk sending their child to Limbo by leaving him unbaptized for ten months?

Back out in the street, Danny had just turned the corner when he spotted a man across the way who looked, at least from the back, like the Tinker. The man stood in front of a shop, looking absently at the sporting goods on display, and smoking. He wore a scruffy, brown suit jacket and a brown hat. As Danny started across the street, the man caught Danny's reflection in the plate glass window. He spun around, facing Danny for an instant, and took off running.

It was definitely the Tinker.

Danny ran into the street and a blue Morris Minor came to a screeching halt in front of him.

''Watch where you're going, you bleeding idjut,'' the driver screamed, as Danny made it safely to the other side, looking around desperately for the Tinker.

He shoved people out of the way as he pushed his way down the busy sidewalk. He saw the Tinker duck into an alleyway, but by the time he reached the entrance to the alley the Tinker was gone.

Danny ran down the alley, his lungs burning from the exertion. At the end of the alley he caught a glimpse of the Tinker running down another street. He chased after him and finally caught him at the entrance of a printer's shop. He pushed the Tinker against a wall. The Tinker looked at him wildly as he struggled to free himself from the hold Danny had on his coat.

"What d'ye want?" the Tinker shrieked in a heavy brogue, as he twisted to free himself.

"I want to know what you were doing out in Ballycara."

"I don't know what ye're talking about, Yank." The Tinker spat out the last word as if it were bile.

"Don't give me that," Danny said, shaking him. "I have pictures of you out there, and you know it."

The Tinker seemed to relax, as if in defeat. "I didn't kill her," he blurted out.

"Who?" Danny asked, startled.

"The old woman, sure. I didn't kill her."

"You liar," Danny yelled, suddenly enraged.

But the Tinker looked at him with suffering eyes. "Sure, she was dead when I found her."

"When did you find her?"

"It was just a few minutes before you saw me.

We'd been camped out at Kilbaha for several weeks. The rest of them had left the day before, but I'd had trouble with me carburetor. When I was after fixing it, I was driving back to Kilkee. I stopped at the cottage to ask did she have a bit of gas I might borrow. When I went into the yard and knocked at the door there was nobody home. Then I saw her lying in the garden with her head busted in; but I swear before God I didn't do it!''

Danny shook him again in rage, "You liar! What about the purse?''

"Sure, I took the purse. I went into the house after I found her and the purse was sitting there on the table. I took it and got out of there. You can't hang this t'ing on me, Yank.''

"What was in the purse?''

"Couple o' pounds.''

Danny tightened his grip on the Tinker's lapel. "What's your name?''

"Carmody. Paddy Carmody. Sure, I'm just a poor traveler. Never a bit of trouble with the law.''

Danny released the Tinker and pushed him back against the wall. "Well, you're into it up to here now,'' he said, drawing his finger across his throat.

The Tinker straightened his coat. "I didn't kill her. I'll swear before God and all his angels to that.''

"Just robbed her.''

"Sure, a few pounds.''

Danny wasn't sure what to do next. Call the police? Tell Garda Kelley? While he was working it out in his mind, the Tinker swung his massive right fist, knocking Danny's glasses off and catching him in the jaw. Before Danny knew what had happened, he was lying on the ground.

When he came to, he was sitting in a chair in the printer's shop and a cold rag had been placed on his forehead. His jaw ached from the blow and he touched it gently and winced from the pain. After he assured the printer that he was fine, and that the law didn't need to be called, he made his way across town to the Old Ground Hotel.

He slipped a note to the man at the front desk, requesting that guest Mona Noonan meet him downstairs. Then he found a seat in front of the crackling fire in the lobby of the hotel, and managed to get a pot of hot tea, which he sipped.

"You look a bit shaken," Mona Noonan said when she came up and sat across from Danny.

"Cup of tea?" Danny asked, ignoring her remark.

Mona nodded. "What happened to your face?"

"Heredity," Danny answered. "Now, I understand you wanted to tell me something."

"Yes," Mona said, taking a sip of tea and hesitating as if gathering her thoughts. "Mr. O'Flaherty," she began, "may I speak frankly?"

"Of course, and please call me Danny. After all,

we're first cousins twice removed, no?'' Danny already disliked the woman.

"Yes, well. I understand you've taken quite an interest in my mother and her unfortunate death.''

"Of course I have. I've been corresponding with your mother for some time. I was completely shocked by what happened.''

"We've all been shocked. But, despite your interest in your, how shall I put it...roots, this really is no concern of yours.''

Danny looked at her coldly. What did she have to hide, anyway? She seemed indifferent to the death of her mother.

"No concern of mine?'' he asked. "I've been accused of killing her.''

Mona shrugged.

Danny decided to go on the offensive. "That was a curious will your mother wrote.''

"How so?''

"The majority of the land went to Johnny and Mickey Duffey.''

"They've always been close to my mother.''

"Don't you feel cheated?''

Mona Noonan sighed heavily. "Mr. O'Flaherty, why would I feel cheated? I'm not a farmer. It's only right that the farm land go to Johnny and Mickey. I live in Dublin, after all; I've no use for farm land.''

"What was your relationship with your mother like?"

"Mother was an old-fashioned Irish country woman. I am a modern, well-educated, well-traveled Dubliner. We disagreed on nearly everything."

"What about the house? What do you intend to do with it?"

"Sell it, if that's possible. But there aren't many people who wish to live in the west of Ireland, despite whatever conclusions you've drawn about our quaint society."

"I wasn't aware that I'd drawn any conclusions."

"You're a Yank. I'm sure you find it all romantic, as if we're a bunch of noble savages. You know, whitewashed cottages, pigs in the parlor, leprechauns, that class of thing. Have you confirmed all the preconceptions you arrived with? You wouldn't think to go to Dublin where over a third of the Irish people live. Too much reality there for you."

Danny's face burned with indignation. "Why did you want to meet me here?"

"I've informed Garda Kelley that he has absolutely no reason to detain you, nor to continue pursuing you in his investigation. That man is an idiot, as I'm sure you've gathered. It's clear that you had nothing to do with my mother's death. And so, Mr.

O'Flaherty, I really think it's best that you return to your *own* country.''

"Did your mother have any enemies?"

Mona winced. "I've no idea, of course.''

"Where were you between nine and ten on Saturday?"

Mona smiled. "I was at my office.''

"On Saturday?"

"My assistant had made a horrible mess of the accounts and I spent my weekend straightening things out.''

"Anybody see you?"

"The office is closed on Saturday. I was alone.''

"I see,'' said Danny.

"Mr. O'Flaherty, please. Leave the detective work to our *Garda Siochana,* and go back to *your* country.''

"Well, Cousin,'' Danny said. "I have no intention of returning to my country until I've gotten to the bottom of this murder. I think there's something being covered up around here and I want to know what.''

"Why? What concern of yours is it?"

"Curiosity.''

"You know what they say, Mr. O'Flaherty?"

"What's that?"

"Curiosity killed the cat.''

# TEN

DANNY'S BRUISED JAW was the topic of much discussion the next day at Larkin's Pub.

"Sure, it's well-known you've your eye on Fidelma Muldoon," said Brendan Grady. "You must have tried some of your stuff on her to earn yourself that jaw."

Seamus Larkin and Tim Mahoney laughed gleefully.

But Danny was in no mood for jokes. He sat alone at the bar, staring into his pint of Harp and thinking about what he should do about Paddy Carmody. For some reason he actually believed the Tinker. Why would he kill a harmless old woman for the few pounds in her purse? Perhaps she *was* already dead when he happened by the farm. Besides, Seamus Larkin's alibi had proved to be a lie; why did he claim to be at Harris Brothers in Kilkee at the time of the murder? What was he trying to hide?

According to Mrs. Slattery, Seamus Larkin lived with his mother in a small apartment above the pub. He had spent fifteen years working in the building trades in England, supporting his mother all the while. He had never married, and was driven by a single-minded desire to buy a pub in Ballycara, which he had accomplished just five years before. By the standards of the village, Seamus Larkin was a worldly man, and he enjoyed his status. He was driven now, it seemed, by money. Not that there was much to buy in the village. According to Mrs. Slattery, he wanted money only for the sense of superiority that it gave him over his fellow villagers. Danny O'Flaherty thought Seamus Larkin was a queer one, indeed.

Danny rubbed his jaw and thought again of the problem of Paddy Carmody. The right thing to do would be to tell Garda Kelley what he had learned. But how could he do that without telling him about the purse? Picking up the purse was a mistake Danny regretted.

"Another one?" Larkin asked, cocking his head at the nearly empty pint in front of Danny.

"Yeah," Danny said, barely able to respond from the pain in his jaw.

Larkin drew another pint of Guinness for Tim Mahoney and set it on the drain board for the head to settle. Then he drew a pint of Harp for Danny, wiped the place in front of him with a rag and set the jar of lager before him.

"So, are you telling how you got the sore jaw or no?"

Danny took a sip of Harp and eyed Larkin.

"Yeah. I'll tell you. Why don't you call Garda Kelley down here? I think it's a story he'd like to hear."

"That good, is it?" Tim Mahoney said from across the room.

"That good," said Danny.

"I'll go get him myself," Brendan Grady said, putting his hat on and rushing out the door.

When he returned with Kelley, the garda looked at Danny disdainfully and asked, "What's this all about, so?"

"I think I know who murdered Rose," Danny said.

Garda Kelley flipped his notebook open with a flourish. "A confession is it?"

Danny ignored the remark. He reached into his pocket and withdrew the picture of the Tinker. "Ever see this man?" Danny asked the garda.

Garda Kelley took the picture and inspected it. "Can't say that I have."

"Name's Paddy Carmody. I saw him coming from the direction of Rose's house on the day of the murder."

Danny related the events in Ennis of the day before. "He gave me a good smack on the jaw before he ran away." Danny rubbed his jaw. "I'd say, even if he's not your man, it would be a good idea to pick him up and ask him some questions."

Kelley seemed both fascinated and annoyed. He

was probably angry that the Yank was showing him up in front of the other villagers. He didn't want to admit that Danny had actually found out more than he had about the murder.

"How do I know you're not just trying to shift the blame from yourself, Mr. O'Flaherty?"

"You don't. That's probably why it's a good idea to talk to Paddy Carmody."

Garda Kelley shifted uncomfortably.

"And I have the purse," Danny said impulsively, both relieved that he had finally let it out, and already regretting it.

"You?" Kelley eyed him suspiciously.

"That's right," and Danny related how he had come by the purse. "I'll walk you over to my car and give it to you now."

"This won't look good for you, O'Flaherty."

Danny shrugged and took a sip of Harp. "I have nothing to hide."

They went across the street and fetched the purse from Danny's rented car. Kelley took notes as Danny explained once again the circumstances by which he had gotten the purse, exactly where he had found it, and when.

"This will not," Garda Kelley repeated, "go well for you, Yank."

Danny was sure that it wouldn't. But Carmody had to be taken into custody, even if only for the robbery.

"I guess that all depends on what you find out from Carmody."

"We'll see," said Kelley.

Danny returned to the pub. He was glad to have come clean about the purse. With Kelley on the trail of the Tinker, Danny could concentrate on other suspects. Liam Flynn was still a possibility. Danny needed to find out where Seamus Larkin had been at the time of the murder. He was convinced that Larkin had more to do with Rose's death than the Tinker. As for the rest of the villagers, according to Mrs. Slattery, most were at Mass at the time of the murder.

After another pint of stout, Tim Mahoney said to Danny, "When are we going out to have a look at the ring fort on the Pinkerton estate?"

"Today's as good a day as any," Danny said.

"We're off then," said Mahoney, swallowing the last of his stout and waving goodbye to Seamus and Brendan.

Danny and Tim walked out of the pub and across the street to Danny's car. Although the day was sunny, dark clouds were moving in from the Atlantic.

"You know we've fierce gales in these parts," Tim told him. "They blow the roofs off the houses, sure."

Danny started the car and swung around in the direction of Kilbaha. A farmer was driving a pack of sheep across the road; Danny stopped to let the flock pass. Despite their reputation, sheep really were ugly things, Danny thought. Their wool was a dirty gray and hunks of dung clung to their backsides.

"What exactly is a stone fort?" Danny asked Tim.

"Well, we're not sure precisely," Tim began pedantically. "Some are merely enclosures that marked spots of religious significance. Built as far back as twelve hundred BC, ring forts are called *raths* when they are made of earth or clay, and *cahers* when they are made of stone. These were probably compounds which early people used as much to corral animals as for fortifications. But there's a lot of speculation about that."

"Who were these people?"

"Prehistoric people who lived in daub and wattle huts."

"Celts?"

"No, the Celts did not start to dominate the native tribes until around six hundred BC, but once they were established they completely overcame the native inhabitants. Of course, the Celts had their own language, laws, and religion."

Tim Mahoney's voice grew pontifical as he warmed to his subject. "I heard a professor from Galway saying that in east Clare the area was an oak forest. When it came to the bronze age, the people started coming down from north Clare every summer. They would bring everything they had with them: the whole extended family, plus their animals. Every family would set up, and they'd put this wall of stones around their things. And when it came to the winter time they would go up again to north Clare, because it was warmer up there because of all the stones in the Burren. There was grass for their animals. Nothing would die of the hunger in it. Even though Cromwell said 'there wasn't water enough to drown a man, wood enough to hang a man, or earth enough to bury a man,' yet the people were wealthy up there in the Burren.''

Danny shifted into high and sped along the pockmarked road. The sun played hide-and-seek behind the clouds, and Tim Mahoney talked on. Danny not so much listened as let the musical cadences of the language wash over him.

''Ring forts are usually found in closely set pairs or groups of forts. Another interesting fact is that no other kind of tree,'' Tim was saying, ''will grow in the ring forts but whitethorn trees. Only whitethorn. You'd never find an oak, or an ash tree. Only whitethorn. I don't know why. That's something I'd love to ask a horticulturist.''

''Yes,'' Danny said absently. But his mind was still on the murder of Rose. Despite what he had told Garda Kelley, he felt certain that Paddy Carmody had not killed Rose. By the same token, Seamus Larkin did not seem in the least suspicious in his behavior or his speech. It was only in the lie that he had been at Harris Brothers at the time of the murder that he showed any inconsistency at all. And Mona Noonan had certainly acted strangely. Why was she so anxious for Danny to get out of the country? Had she something to hide?

"You must never cut," Tim was saying passionately, "one of those whitethorn trees encircling a ring fort. But if it fell, you'd bring it home and burn it; but, if you cut one down intentionally, sure you won't have an ounce of luck in your house after that."

"You believe that?" Danny asked, his mind switching reluctantly back to Tim.

"Sure, I have to believe it. I know too many stories about people who disturbed the ring forts. There was a terrible thing happened in our own parish when they decided to build a new rectory for the priest. Now where Father O'Malley lives over there is a new house. That was built maybe thirteen, fourteen years ago. Well, the first priest that moved into that house was there about a fortnight and he died. They got another priest. He said one First Friday Mass and *he* died. And the third priest came and he ordered two lovely statues of our Lord and our Lady from Italy and he had gone to get them. He was on his way home from Galway and didn't he go in under a truck and was killed. But he didn't die until the eighth of December—the Feast of the Immaculate Conception—showing the devotion he had to Our Lady. All the old people said that house shouldn't have been built there because it was on the direct line between one ring fort and another about a quarter of a mile away. They said that the fairies moved up and down there and it was a pathway between the two forts, and that there would never be any luck in that house.''

"Has anything happened since?"

"No, the three priests died, which was very strange like. But I don't think there's been any terrible bad luck since then. But it's very hard to get a priest to come here."

"Mrs. Slattery also says that it's dangerous to mess around with ring forts."

"Loads of people believe that."

"Do you?"

"Sure, she may be right," Tim said evasively. "There are so many of the dead buried in those places."

Danny drove over a narrow bridge that spanned a stream and Tim pointed to the two imposing stone pillars that held a wrought iron gate.

"Drive in through there. We'll park at the Pinkerton estate and see would old Peadar MacGreevy take us out to the stone fort."

The gate was open and Danny drove between

the pillars. A long unpaved road ran beneath two columns of sycamore trees. On both sides of the avenue of trees were fields of well-kept hay where horses and cattle munched on the sumptuous grasses. At the end of the long driveway Danny could see a large Georgian manor house set on several acres of garden. Although the house looked as though it needed some work, and the garden was overgrown, the house was, without a doubt, a fine example of an Anglo-Irish dwelling.

"When was it built?" Danny asked, marveling at the beautiful residence.

"Jeremiah Pinkerton built Trelawny in the eighteenth century. You met George Pinkerton at the pub. He's Jeramiah's eldest son's only son's elder son's elder son. You see, the house passes down through the eldest son. Primogeniture, it is."

Danny parked the car in front of a small cottage to the west of the main residence and Tim got out. Old Peadar MacGreevy came from around the side of the house with a rake in his hand. He was dressed as he had been at the pub: Wellingtons, green canvas pants, and a wool jacket. He neither waved nor smiled, but walked directly up to Tim Mahoney.

"Peadar," Tim greeted him. "We thought we'd come out and have a look at the ring fort. Sure, the Yank here has never seen one."

MacGreevy grunted noncommittally and stood the rake against the wall of the cottage.

Danny turned off the ignition, stepped out, and began to lock the door.

"What are you doing?" asked Tim Mahoney, laughing. "Do you think you're out with a bunch of blackguards?"

Danny looked at the keys in his hand. He did feel foolish, but habits were hard to break, especially that one. As a sign of good faith he tossed the keys absently on the front seat and slammed the door.

"How's your son doing in Dublin, Peadar?" asked Tim.

The old man's face broke into a smile. "Jamie's fine, sure. Works too hard, though. I'm still hoping someday he'll come home."

Peadar MacGreevy motioned with his head for them to follow. He opened a gate behind the manor house that let them into the back pasture. A couple of cows looked up apathetically and returned to their munching.

The back pasture was on high ground; Danny could see for some distance the countryside in three directions—fields of hay to the north and east and the open Atlantic to the west. As if for the first time, he realized how close they were to the O'Flaherty farm. He could actually see Rose's house down in the valley across the meadow.

Danny drew up alongside Peadar MacGreevy while Tim Mahoney strayed behind, occasionally stopping to look closely at a wildflower or examine a stone.

"You work for George Pinkerton?" Danny asked conversationally.

MacGreevy nodded.

Danny pointed in the direction of Rose's place. "I don't suppose you saw anyone going down there the day Rose was killed?"

The old man shook his head.

"Did you ever sell turf to Liam Flynn?"

"Sure," the old man answered laconically. Then he added, "Every year for the past six or seven."

"You cut the turf?"

"It's cut by machine, Mr. O'Flaherty."

"How long have you worked for Mr. Pinkerton?"

"All me life."

"Do you like working here?"

"Sure, I wouldn't be here if I didn't."

"Where were you between say nine and ten last Saturday morning?"

Peadar McGreevy hesitated for a moment, then said, "Betsy was calving at the time and I was after checking up on her."

"Betsy?"

"One of the cows."

"Anybody with you?"

"I've no help here a-tall, Mr. O'Flaherty, as you can see. Sure, I was by myself."

"Where was Mr. Pinkerton?"

"I've no idea. He has other affairs to attend to beside the birthing of cattle."

"Does he ever help you?"

"Sometimes."

"Yet he wasn't helping you with the calf?"

"We'd been up most of the night. He was tired, sir, and perhaps had gone to his bed."

"What time was the calf born?" Danny asked.

"She was not."

"Pardon me?"

"Sure, the poor thing couldn't do it. The cow died in labor, along with her calf."

Danny fell silent. What was he doing cross-examining this harmless old man? He started to apologize, but instead he asked: "Did you hear a loud scream that morning?"

"When?"

"Saturday morning."

Peadar MacGreevy looked at him oddly. "I heard no scream at all on Saturday."

They came to the circle of stones after a ten minute walk.

"I've done some cleaning around it," Tim Mahoney said proudly. "When I first discovered the fort, it was so overgrown with bushes and trees, you wouldn't recognize it as a stone fort at all."

Eighteen large stones had been placed in a circle about twenty or thirty feet in diameter. There was something oddly peaceful to Danny about the setting and he tried, without success, to imagine the kind of people who had put up these stones.

But Danny could not concentrate on the stone fort despite the lengthy lecture Tim Mahoney delivered. Danny was thinking about Mona Noonan. She insisted that Danny had no business investigating the murder of her mother, which might have been true. But how else could he prove he hadn't done it?

WHEN DANNY got back to Shannonside, Mrs. Slattery was in her usual place, saying her beads in the rocker in front of the fire while the TV blared.

Danny joined her.

"Where were you all day?" she asked.

"Off looking at ring forts with Tim Mahoney."

"Ah, yes, the fairy forts."

Danny told her what had happened in Ennis and that he had reported it to Garda Kelley. "Do you know Mona Noonan very well?" he asked Mrs. Slattery.

"Sure, I've known Mona her whole life. I assisted the midwife when she was born."

"I talked to Mona in Ennis yesterday."

"Yes."

"I hate to say this," Danny began, "but she seemed awfully rude."

"Mona? I can't believe it. Why she's the sweetest person you could imagine. Kind, thoughtful. Always thinking of the other person and not a bit of herself."

Danny shook his head. He could hardly believe they were talking about the same person.

# ELEVEN

DANNY SLEPT LATE the next morning. When he came downstairs, to his surprise, Fidelma Muldoon was waiting for him in the parlor with Mrs. Slattery.

"Danny," Fidelma said, with concern in her voice. She rose from her chair and moved toward him, touching him on the cheek with her hand. "I heard you were hurt."

"Just a scrape," Danny said bravely, enjoying the attention. He suddenly remembered that today was the wake and Rosary service for Rose. Tomorrow would be the funeral.

"I found out something," Fidelma said in a low voice so that Mrs. Slattery, who was across the room dusting, could not hear. "It's about Paddy Carmody."

Danny looked at her swiftly and led her to a chair beside the fire. "What is it?" he asked.

"You're too late for your breakfast, Mr. O'Flaherty," Mrs. Slattery shouted across the room.

Danny glanced quickly at his watch. "Guess I slept a bit late this morning."

"A bit late," Mrs. Slattery repeated. "Sure, it's almost two o'clock in the afternoon." She disappeared into the kitchen.

Danny turned to Fidelma, who looked at him with twinkling eyes. A strand of red hair had fallen across her forehead and she brushed it aside quickly. The ache in Danny's jaw seemed to dissipate as he looked at the smooth skin of her face, the lobes of her ears that held tiny gold rings, and her wet lips like a small pink mollusk.

"What is it?" he asked expectantly.

"Paddy Carmody was arrested in Ennis yesterday. They're holding him at the barracks there."

"Really. How do you know?"

"Father O'Malley was in Ennis this morning and brought back a paper." Fidelma handed him a clipping from *The Clare Champion:*

### Suspect Arrested

Gardai were called to arrest Paddy Carmody of Ennis, County Clare. He is being questioned in connection with the murder and robbery of Rose Noonan, in Ballycara. No charges have been filed, though a preliminary background check revealed that Carmody is also sought for questioning by authorities in Northern Ireland on unspecified charges.

Fidelma threw her arms around Danny and hugged him. "So there," she said. "They've got their murderer and Garda Kelley can stop hounding you. And *you* solved it for them!"

"He didn't do it."

"What?"

"Paddy Carmody didn't kill Rose. I'm sure of it."

Fidelma looked crestfallen. "What makes you so sure?"

"Well, I don't know exactly."

"I thought," Fidelma snickered, "you were sure."

Danny bristled. "I'm sure he didn't do it. I'm just not sure how I know. Besides, why do you suppose Seamus Larkin was lying about being at Harris Brothers at the time of the murder?"

"You're the sleuth," Fidelma said, "not me."

"And I'll get to the bottom of it, mind you."

Fidelma slouched back in her chair, pouting. "Oh, you. You *want* to keep worrying about this. Even on the day of poor Rose's wake." She took out a tissue and dabbed at her eyes. "God rest her soul."

Mrs. Slattery came in from the kitchen with a platter of tea and scones. "What's this now?" she asked, having overheard only part of the argument. Then she saw Fidelma crying.

"Oh, you poor thing. You did love Rose so." Mrs. Slattery set down the tea things and put her arm around Fidelma. "Rose is in a better place now," she said to Fidelma. "Sure, she's at the right hand of the Father, with all the saints and angels around her. She's looking down on all of us now."

Fidelma dabbed her eyes and gave a weak smile. She took a cup of tea and blew on the hot liquid before taking a sip.

Danny nibbled at a scone and sucked loudly on his tea.

"We'll go over to the funeral parlor at three and sit with Rose for a while. The Rosary's at six."

"When's the funeral Mass?" Danny asked.

"Tomorrow morning at half-nine. Then they'll take her out to the family plot at Killballyowen Cemetery."

The three of them sipped their tea quietly, hardly speaking. Danny gave Fidelma's arm a weak squeeze and she smiled at him, crinkling her red-rimmed eyes.

Danny drove the rental car with Fidelma in front beside him and Mrs. Slattery in back. They stopped on the outskirts of Ballycara to pick up an ancient crony of Mrs. Slattery who lived by herself in a house just outside of town. When they had collected Mrs. McGinty they drove into Kilkee.

Danny had been expecting an Irish wake in the home, with drunken relations and the whole lot, but that practice had disappeared some years ago.

The funeral home, though somewhat shabby, was little different than the O'Flaherty Funeral Parlor in New York that Danny's father had operated.

The undertaker, in his black pinstripe suit, was appropriately grave and shook hands with Danny as they came through the door.

Mrs. Slattery spoke to him as they signed the guest book. "This is Rose's cousin from the states, Danny O'Flaherty."

"Ah, sure," he said, patting Danny on the shoulder, "Sean's grandson."

"No," Mrs. Slattery corrected. "Daniel P. O'Flaherty's."

"Of course." The undertaker took him up to sit on the right side of the aisle with Mona Noonan and Johnny and Mickey Duffey. Mrs. Slattery sat on the left side. "Sit with me, would you?" he asked Fidelma suddenly.

"I will."

Rose O'Flaherty Noonan lay in repose beneath a spray of roses, carnations, and assorted wreaths. Danny and Fidelma approached the open casket, knelt on the white kneeler in front of the casket, and blessed themselves.

Rose's hands were folded atop her midsection with a set of rosary beads intertwined in her fingers. Looking at her, serene and worry-free in the casket, Danny pictured her as she was the morning he found her. That seemed like years ago, though it was only Saturday. God, what a nightmare it had all become! What was he doing here? He had come to Ireland for some sentimental reason, some way of getting in touch with his parents and his grand-parents. His roots, for God's sake. Now this? A funeral halfway around the world for someone he had never met alive, yet was bound to by the ab-surd tie of blood. Mona Noonan was right. He was a stranger here, engulfed in something now larger than himself. He glanced at Fidelma as she wiped a tear from her eye. He must find out who did this. Perhaps he had not known Rose, but he was sick-ened by her murder.

The blow had been to the back of the head. Rose's head now rested on a pillow. No wound was visible and her hair and makeup made her look not alive, only life-like. Danny felt the tears well-ing up. He was not sure exactly who he was crying for—his father, his mother, his grandfather, Rose, or himself.

Fidelma blessed herself and rose from the kneeler. Danny followed her as if in a trance, and they pushed in beside Johnny and Mickey Duffey. They knelt and prayed briefly, then sat back in the pew as people came up to view the body and offer their condolences. Danny gave Fidelma's hand a squeeze.

Mona Noonan stood to the right of the coffin, dressed in a dark suit. There's something not quite right with her, Danny thought, as she embraced a weeping villager. She seemed threatened by Danny's investigation of the murder. Why should she be? You'd think she'd be glad to have the murderer brought to justice, no matter who accomplished it. She also seemed too satisfied with the will. After all, the tiny house she inherited would probably be worth less than the land Johnny and Mickey were given. Was she really as kind and unselfish as Mrs. Slattery said she was? Or did she have something to hide? Motive? She herself admitted in their conversation at the Old Ground Hotel that she and her mother disagreed on nearly everything. Opportunity? Ireland's a small country. She could have gotten from Dublin to Ballycara and back in a day's time. Alibi? She was working at her office on a Saturday, alone. It couldn't be substantiated. Yes, Mona Noonan's an odd one, Danny thought.

Liam Flynn hobbled up to the casket, his rosary beads dangling from his hands. He knelt in front of the body, his lips moving in prayer. Flynn had loved Rose, Danny remembered. Or did he? He loved the land she lived on more than anything, it seemed to him. But was that really a motive? Kill her for the land? If so, it didn't do him any good. Johnny and Mickey Duffey would have the land. What about a lover's quarrel? He had asked her to marry him countless times and she refused. But could a man his age possibly kill a woman because she had refused his love? Preposterous! But it was his *slane* that killed her, he admitted to that. Opportunity? He had been there within minutes after Danny found her. Said he was going over to ask her to sell the land. That's what bothered Danny about Liam Flynn; he was too transparent, everything up front. Either he was an incredibly smooth liar, everything in plain view where one least expects to find it, or an innocent old man.

Tim Mahoney approached the coffin, obviously grieving. He wiped a tear from his eye and blessed himself, murmuring Rose's name. Tim Mahoney seemed the least capable of anyone of murder. Yet he certainly had the opportunity. He had been at the ring fort taking measurements at the time Rose was murdered. The ring fort was no more than a five minute walk across Pinkerton's pasture to Rose's house. Yet he claimed he saw no one coming or going from Rose's house that morning. Not even Paddy Carmody. But what possible motive would Tim Mahoney have? It was hard to figure him, really, Danny thought. As friendly as he was, there was something elusive about him. He rarely talked about himself, or anyone else, for that matter. It was always ring forts, local history, superstitions, that sort of thing. Perhaps it was his way of drawing attention away from himself. I need to watch him more closely, Danny concluded.

George Pinkerton seemed out of place at the Rosary. He held his hands awkwardly at his sides, then folded them for a second, then let them drop to his sides again. Every time Danny had seen Pinkerton since coming to Ballycara, he had been the picture of confidence and self-control—a man who knew who and what he was. Here he looked like— Danny thought of what his mother might say—a fish out of water. But he was quite simply a Protestant at a Catholic Rosary Service, not quite sure what it was all about. He strode stiffly up to Mona Noonan, purposely turning his eyes away from the corpse as if it were something obscene, and shook hands with Mona. Everyone in the village had told Danny that Pinkerton was a decent man, and they seemed to like him. Danny had no reason to believe otherwise. Yet it was well known that he, too, had been trying to buy out Rose for years. His land adjoined hers. He could expand the Pinkerton estate. But none of that added up. Rose had been killed; her will specified Johnny and Mickey and Mona as heirs, and that was that. He had no motive that Danny could see. Opportunity? Peadar MacGreevy said that Pinkerton was in the house at the time of the murder. They had been up all night trying to help the cow give birth. He could have gone to his bedroom, locked the door, slipped out a window, walked across the field to Rose's house. Oh, Danny thought in exasperation, that's really stretching it. George Pinkerton was as innocent as a lamb.

Peadar MacGreevy came up behind his employer, better dressed than Danny had ever seen him. He wore a dark blue suit that looked as though it had seen the light of day only on the rare occasions of weddings and funerals. He himself would probably be buried in it, Danny thought, in the not-too-distant future. MacGreevy knelt and murmured a short prayer in front of the coffin. He was not a talkative man, Danny remembered. There was something slightly suspicious about him, but Lord, at his age, he hardly looked to have enough strength to pick up a *slane,* much less bash Rose in the back of the head with it. He claimed to have been taking care of the pregnant cow at the time of the murder. Would Pinkerton vouch for that? Danny must ask him. Again, there was opportunity, but no apparent motive. Keep checking, Danny said to himself.

Brendan Grady was an interesting one, Danny thought as he saw him approach the coffin. Grady looked no different here at the funeral home than he did back at Larkin's Pub—same clothes, same casual way of walking. He stepped up to the coffin as if he were stepping up to the bar for another Guinness. He looked down at Rose and smiled. Smiled? Was that an appropriate gesture under the circumstances? Danny wondered. Grady said that he had overslept the morning Rose was killed. They had all been drinking until late at Larkin's, and Grady had slept until two o'clock Saturday afternoon. He lived with his father and his sister. They could verify that, if need be. He probably had less opportunity to murder Rose than some of the others. Motive? Brendan Grady was a mystery man. He had IRA connections. And something about the clipping Fidelma gave Danny this morning made him wonder. It said that Paddy Carmody was wanted for questioning in Northern Ireland. Maybe Danny was naive, but whenever he thought of Northern Ireland all he could think of was the IRA. Was it possible that Brendan Grady was somehow connected to Paddy Carmody? Could Rose's murder somehow be IRA business? Then there was that rumor about an old grudge between Brendan Grady's family and Danny's grandfather. What about Rose's father? Danny wondered. Had he been involved in the rebellion as well? Brendan Grady was another one that needed to be watched more closely, Danny concluded.

Which left whom? Paddy Carmody, in jail in Ennis. He wasn't the man, Danny was sure of it, though he deserved time for robbing her.

Seamus Larkin moved up the aisle toward the coffin, toward the flowers. He wore the same scowl on his face that he wore in the pub. Larkin did not seem like an unhappy man, Danny thought. He seemed like he enjoyed being miserable, and making other people miserable. How strange that he should have become a publican.

Seamus Larkin stood briefly in front of the casket, looking down at Rose. Danny almost expected him to make some derisive remark to the corpse. There was no doubt in Danny's mind that of all the residents of Ballycara, Seamus Larkin had the temperament for murder, though Danny could not pinpoint one specific motive. Larkin seemed to hate everyone in the village, and seemed to carry a private grudge against everyone he knew. He had lied about being at Harris Brothers in order to cover something, that was clear. It was the specific hour between nine and ten o'clock on Saturday that he was trying to cover for. It would be just like Seamus Larkin to use Liam Flynn's *slane* in order to cast blame on poor Flynn. Liam Flynn said that he had not noticed the *slane* was missing for some time. Larkin may have taken the *slane* months ago, planning all along how he would use it.

The way Danny figured it, Larkin had slipped out early Saturday morning with the *slane* in the boot of his car. He may have hidden the car somewhere near Rose's house and walked across the fields to her place. Would he have known she would be outside at the time? Perhaps he had watched her movements. God knows, everyone in this community seemed to know everything there was to know about each other. He could have come up behind her as she bent over her flowers. He'd have been wearing gloves to avoid leaving prints. The fact that Danny had picked up the *slane* was just a stroke of luck for Larkin. He had raised the slane over his head and...bang!

Danny shuddered violently and Fidelma reached out and touched his arm.

"It's all right," she consoled. "Like Mrs. Slattery said, she's in a better place now."

Danny smiled at her weakly. Seamus Larkin blessed himself and turned away from the coffin. Clearly he was the one, Danny concluded. It made the most sense. Maybe the Tinker, Paddy Carmody, and he were in it together somehow, or maybe that part of it was just coincidence, but Danny was sure that Seamus Larkin had a hand in it. The man looked positively evil. And he was probably the one who had broken into Danny's room and taken the letter, which meant that he feared there was something in that letter to implicate him. Something about the information Rose was to give Danny about his grandfather? He killed her, Danny was sure. All Danny needed to figure out now was *why* he killed her.

All afternoon the villagers came to pay their last respects to Rose O'Flaherty Noonan. Even Garda Kelley was there in his bright blue uniform and cap, with the silver buttons on his uniform gleaming under the fluorescent light of the funeral home.

At six o'clock, Father O'Malley arrived and stood at the podium that was raised on a platform behind the casket. The people knelt and fingered their beads as Father O'Malley took his missal from the pocket of his cassock and made the sign of the cross.

"Glory be to the Father, and to the Son, and to the Holy Spirit, as it was in the beginning, is now, and ever shall be, world without end, amen."

# TWELVE

"In the name of the Father, and of the Son, and of the Holy Spirit."

Father O'Malley began the funeral Mass for Rose O'Flaherty Noonan the next morning at nine-thirty.

Enough of the renovations on the church had been completed to have the funeral Mass in the church in Ballycara. Danny and Fidelma sat together with Mona, Johnny and Mickey Duffey, and some other relatives who had come in that morning from England, though Danny had not yet met them formally. Danny felt as though he had been in church for half of the time he had been in Ireland, and the rest of the time in the pub. The Rosary had ended about seven o'clock the night before and he had driven Mrs. McGinty and Mrs. Slattery home and dropped off Fidelma at the rectory. She had invited him in for a cup of tea and they had sat talking quietly.

Danny did not tell her yet that he believed Seamus Larkin was responsible for the murder. He wanted solid evidence of it, then he would announce it to the whole village, with Garda Kelley present.

He could just imagine the policeman's face as Danny explained why and how the murder had been accomplished.

Danny and Fidelma talked only about Rose. He felt surprisingly close to Fidelma given that they had only known each other for a week. But she was perhaps too reserved, Danny thought. There was a part of her that was inaccessible to him and whenever he came too close she seemed to close off inside.

"You have called your servant, Rose, from this life..." Danny heard Father O'Malley intoning, "save her from final damnation..." and while Danny's mind wandered for the next hour over all of the events that had taken place since he had arrived in Ireland, "and count her among those you have chosen..." The Mass ended and Danny and Fidelma piled out of the church with the rest of the congregation.

"Shall we go to the cemetery?" Fidelma asked him.

Mrs. Slattery had followed them out of the church and stood next to Fidelma.

"I don't think I'll go," Mrs. Slattery said wearily. "Sure, I'll just walk back to Shannonside."

"Are you sure?" asked Fidelma.

"Yes, yes. You two go ahead. Poor Rose," she mumbled almost incoherently.

"Shall we bring you out to the house afterward?" Danny asked.

"No, no. I've said my good-byes now, God rest her soul. Sure, it won't be long before I'm joining her," Mrs. Slattery sighed.

"Don't be silly," Fidelma consoled her, squeezing her arm. "We'll drop you off on our way out."

"No, go ahead. I can walk home."

Danny and Fidelma got into the rental car and followed the procession of automobiles out of the village toward Killballyowen Cemetery. They parked beneath a beech tree and walked up to the graveyard. A small knot of people were crowded around the freshly-dug grave, which was just behind Danny's great-grandmother's grave. Danny and Fidelma paused before it.

"This would be Rose's grandmother's grave," Danny said, looking down at his great-grandmother's tombstone.

Fidelma squeezed his hand and urged him toward the casket that stood under a green tent. Father O'Malley read briefly from his missal, sprayed the casket with holy water, and blessed it. "O God," he concluded, "the Creator and Redeemer of all the faithful, grant to the soul of Thy departed servant, Rose O'Flaherty Noonan, the remission of all her sins, that through pious supplication she may obtain that pardon which she has always desired: Who livest and reignest forever and ever. May she rest in peace. Amen.''

Fidelma sniffled and Danny bravely held back the tears. At that moment a few drops of rain pelted the roof of the tent, and Mona Noonan popped open a bright red umbrella over her head and stepped away from the grave toward her car.

Fidelma whimpered, and as Danny turned to her she fell into his arms, at last giving into the torrent of grief that she had reserved since the day of Rose's death. Danny held her close and rocked her as she shuddered in his arms and patted the back of her hair softly.

"Poor, dear Rose," Fidelma murmured. "Damn the person who did this," she hissed with uncharacteristic vehemence.

"Don't worry," Danny said, kneading the back of her neck. "He is damned already."

The knot of people broke up abruptly as a soft rain misted over the graveyard. Danny shivered and pulled Fidelma closer to him as they made their way back to the car. He turned on his headlights and followed the car in front of him in the direction of Rose's house.

"She was such a darling woman," Fidelma said to Danny. "It's a shame you never knew her."

"Yes," Danny said absently.

"Why," Fidelma asked, her voice choking with emotion, "why?"

"I don't know. But I really will find out."

Fidelma had brought a plate of sliced Limerick ham covered in waxed paper; she handed it to Mona Noonan, who met them at the door of Rose's house.

"Thank you," Mona said to Fidelma, but she glared at Danny. "Thank you for coming."

Mona put the plate of ham on a table overloaded with food in the back of the room.

Danny looked around curiously. He had not yet been inside Rose's house. It was as though he had just arrived in Ireland. He almost expected Rose to come out of the bedroom and offer him tea in front of the fireplace and tell stories about his grandfather, as if all that had *really* happened between the day Danny arrived in Ireland and this very moment was just a bad dream.

Most of the people that had been at the funeral Mass were at the house. Fidelma led Danny back to the kitchen. Four or five bottles of whiskey had been set out on a table with glasses; a dozen brown bottles of stout stood beside them.

Danny poured himself a shot of Bushmills. The mood of the crowd had changed from the dreary tone of the graveyard. Danny saw Brendan Grady out of the corner of his eye, talking animatedly with a middle-aged woman.

Father O'Malley came up behind Danny and put his hand on his shoulder. "So sorry," he said, then poured himself a shot of Jameson. "Will you be going home soon?"

Danny looked around for Fidelma, who had slipped away from him. He saw her in the corner of the room talking to Mona.

"I'm not sure," Danny answered, "when I'll be going home. I'm supposed to fly out Monday. Three days from now."

"Sounds as though they've got their man," Father O'Malley said. "Thank God. What would drive a man like that to murder a poor defenseless woman?"

"Carmody?"

"Aye."

Danny shrugged and the priest moved away to talk with one of his parishioners. Danny held his glass of whiskey as he wandered about the room. The kitchen was small, with an ancient gas range against one wall, an apartment-size refrigerator on a low table against another wall, and a small sink, with leaky pipes. Danny noted the aluminum bucket beneath it to catch the drip. The table upon which the whiskey bottles sat must have been Rose's dining room table. On the wall above it was a portrait of Our Lady of Prague, the little doll-like saint, to whom Danny's own mother had been devoted.

Danny refilled his glass and moved out of the kitchen into the less crowded living room. On the mantle over the fire was a family portrait of Rose with her deceased husband and her daughter Mona, at about age ten. He looked at the portrait carefully. Rose had been a beautiful woman, Danny thought. He moved about the room looking at the furnishings, noting the few books spread about, a stack of magazines—*Ireland's Own*—on a windowsill.

A short hall connected the living room to another room on the right, the door of which was closed (it must have been Rose's bedroom), and a room to the left. A full-length mirror hung on the right side of the hall; looking into it, Danny could see Seamus Larkin talking on the phone in the room to the left, which was made up like a study. On the left wall of the hall was a gallery of family photographs: Rose and her husband and Mona; some school pictures of Mona alone; wedding pictures of Rose; Mona's First Communion; a picture of Johnny and Mickey as young men.

Danny scanned the gallery of pictures, fascinated. Then one caught his eye. It was an old photograph in an antique frame. A man and woman stood together, dressed in clothes clearly from the 19th century. In front of them stood three children, a boy on the left, a girl, and a boy on the right. Danny peered at the picture and glanced in the mirror quickly to see Seamus Larkin with his back to him, talking excitedly on the phone.

The man and woman must be Rose's grandparents, Danny concluded, my great-grandparents. One of those children would be my grandfather. Danny studied the picture carefully, trying to see a resemblance between the old man he remembered as his grandfather and one of these small boys. Danny looked around, back into the mirror again (Larkin seemed angry), and lifted the picture off the wall and turned it over. On the back, in a nearly faded, florid script had been handwritten:

*Grandma & Grandpa O'Flaherty, 1900,*
*my father Sean O'Flaherty,*
*my Aunt Maureen O'Flaherty, and Daniel P.*

Yes, Danny almost shouted, my grandfather! He flipped the picture back over and replaced it on the wall. He looked into his grandfather's eyes. Who would ever think, Danny began to wonder, but again an inexplicable emotion welled up in him and he bit back tears. All these years, all these miles. He shook his head. He could hear Seamus Larkin's voice rising in the study. He turned to the mirror and watched Larkin, completely undetected.

"It's the way he looks at me," he heard Larkin mutter.

Danny moved closer to the door. He glanced down the hall where Liam Flynn had cornered Father O'Malley and was shouting something into the priest's ear. Danny turned back to the wall of photographs so that no one would detect that he was spying on Seamus Larkin, but moved even closer to the open door so that he could hear him better.

"He knows!" Larkin said loudly, then lowered his voice. "He's asking questions all around like Sherlock Holmes."

Danny's heart pounded. Was he hearing correctly?

A shout rose from Father O'Malley and Danny looked up sharply as the priest pounded Liam Flynn on the back, laughing uproariously. "Grand, grand!" roared the priest.

Danny studied another photograph with feigned interest.

"Don't worry?" Larkin asked incredulously. "Sure, you must be joking."

"There's your roots," someone shouted from down the hall and Danny nearly jumped out of his skin. Danny took a deep breath, trying to calm his racing pulse, and smiled weakly. It was Tim Mahoney, wagging his finger at the wall of photographs. "Take a good look, Danny Boy," Mahoney said. "Those are your roots." Tim threw back a slug of whiskey and moved off toward the kitchen.

Danny rubbed his shaking hand over his forehead and strained to hear Larkin's voice, while trying to look engrossed in the photographs. He was staring at another photo of Rose's grandmother with a child in her arms.

"I can't talk here," Larkin was saying.

Danny looked at the photo.

"Where?" Larkin said softly.

Danny inched closer to the door. Then he remembered the mirror. If he could see Larkin, then Larkin might also turn around, look in the mirror and see him. He glanced back quickly at the mirror, but saw that Larkin still faced away, his back rising and falling with his heavy breathing.

"Tonight?" Larkin nearly shouted. "Kilkee?"

Danny looked at the photograph again. He'd been standing there a bit long, he thought. In order to give his shaking hands something to do, he turned the photo over. On the back, in an even more faded script than the last, he read:

*Our first-born. Sean Michael O'Flaherty, 1893*

"Bayview," he heard Larkin say, "Room Thirteen."

Danny was nauseated from excitement, nerves, the stress of the last two days, the wake, the Rosary, the funeral, the cemetery. Now this.

"Of course, of course," Larkin said. "Nine o'clock. I tell you he knows, for Christ's sake."

Danny looked up and spotted Fidelma at the end

of the hall. He walked briskly toward her, glancing back only briefly as Seamus Larkin came out of the room. Danny guided Fidelma to the kitchen. He was sure he had not been seen.

"What's wrong?" asked Fidelma.

Danny shook his head and reached for the bottle of Bushmills when he got to the kitchen. The bottle was nearly empty. Danny drained it into a glass and threw it back in one gulp.

"Danny!" Fidelma gasped. "What's happened to you?"

Danny's heart pounded. He opened his mouth to speak, but no words came. He grabbed an unopened bottle of Jameson and wrenched the cap off of it. He tried to steady his hands, look calm. Fidelma looked at him as if he were insane.

"Like a drink?" he asked in a squeaky voice that sounded like it belonged to someone else.

Fidelma furrowed her brow. "I do not."

Danny poured himself a generous shot—hell, half a tumbler-full. "Let's get some air," he said.

"I'm thinking you need some," said Fidelma.

She led him through the crowded room, past the table of food. They brushed by Seamus Larkin, who had a piece of soda bread in one hand and was reaching for a slice of the Limerick ham with the other.

Outside, the wind rustled the branches of the beech trees and the smell of the sea blew in from the west. The rain had abated, and the air was cool. The sunlight articulated each leaf of the tree in the yard and lit the green field of clover in front of the house so that it glowed like a bed of emeralds. A raven cawed overhead and circled the house.

Fidelma pointed to it. "Even the birds know she's gone," she said sadly, and she told Danny of the old Irish superstition that if a raven cries around a house it is a sign of death. "You look like you saw a ghost in there," she said, finally.

Danny sucked on his whiskey. He had nearly calmed his nerves, but he was still excited about what he had heard.

"Fidelma," he said, "we need to go to Kilkee tonight."

"What in the world for?"

"I'm sure now who killed Rose."

"Oh, for God's sake," she sighed.

"No, listen. I overheard…" Danny hesitated, afraid almost to say his name, "someone say something very important to my…" Danny hesitated again, "investigation."

Fidelma laughed. "Isn't that a wee bit vague, Inspector O'Flaherty?"

Danny's face burned with indignation. He took a sip of his whiskey. "You come with me to Kilkee tonight, and I will guarantee you that we will know by the end of the night, unequivocally, who murdered Rose."

"Oh, who cares?" Fidelma cried. "Poor Rose is gone now," she said, her voice breaking with emotion. "Finding the blackguard who did this won't bring her back. Why don't you leave all that to Garda Kelley and quit play-acting?"

She pulled a tissue from her pocket and blew her nose.

Danny moved toward Fidelma and put his hand around her shoulder. She was weeping quietly and Danny held her and kissed her cheek. "Fidelma," he said, not sure what he was going to say next. "I've grown very fond of you, you know."

Fidelma stiffened slightly. "Yes?"

Danny wasn't sure where to go with it. "I think you're a very special person..."

"Yes?" Fidelma looked up to him expectantly.

"And I want you to come with me," Danny said in a businesslike tone, "to Kilkee. I'll need a witness for what we're likely to hear and see tonight."

"So that's it," Fidelma said, shrugging away from him. "You need a witness."

Danny wasn't sure whether she was angry or just teasing him. He searched her eyes for a clue.

"What's it all about, Danny?"

"I can't tell you," he said, "just yet."

"Did you see something in there? Did you hear something?"

"Yes."

"Well, what?" Fidelma nearly shouted in exasperation.

"Tonight, in Kilkee," Danny said. "You'll see and hear for yourself. That way you won't make any pre-judgments. You can't say that I made it all up."

"Why all the mystery, Danny?" she said angrily. "This is just a game for you. I *loved* Rose Noonan. And I'd give a million pounds to see whoever did this burn in hell. But I'll not make a game out of this matter a-tall."

Now Danny was the angry one. He grabbed her by the shoulders and shook her slightly. "I'm not playing any games. If Garda Kelley is what you people over here have to rely on as a policeman, then I feel sorry for you Irish." He spit out the last word like a curse. "That idiot will never find out who did this."

Danny's sudden vehemence seemed to calm Fidelma. She put her hand on his cheek and looked at him tenderly. "You do care, don't you?"

"Of course I do."

"What time can you pick me up tonight?"

Danny brightened, looking at her gratefully. "Eight o'clock."

"All right," Fidelma said. "I'll go with you to Kilkee." Then she seemed momentarily angry again. "But this had better not be a wild goose chase."

"It won't be," Danny said. "Trust me."

"Shall we go back inside for a bit longer, then?" said Fidelma.

"Yeah. Let's go back inside."

# THIRTEEN

DANNY PICKED UP Fidelma at the rectory that night at eight o'clock, and they drove in silence toward Kilkee.

Finally, Fidelma asked, slightly annoyed: "When do you intend to tell me what this is all about?"

"You'll see."

To Danny's surprise she did not persist. He thought it would be better if she heard Seamus Larkin condemn himself. As they passed Larkin's Pub, Danny noted the CLOSED sign in the window. My God, he thought, the regulars must be having a fit.

They turned onto the Kilkee road and drove in silence. The air was filled with swirling sea birds batting their wings against the winds blowing off the Atlantic. Danny stole a glance at Fidelma. She stared absently out the window. I wonder if she'd come to see me in New York, he thought suddenly. Perhaps she could fly over and I'd show her the sights of the city.

"Penny for your thoughts," he said, looking at her.

She turned and regarded him for a moment

before speaking. "I was thinking of Rose. Of all the people something like this could happen to...why her?"

Danny wished he knew. But he said nothing. Just before they arrived in Kilkee, Danny briefed Fidelma on part of the plan he had been hatching.

"First," he began, "we are to going to check into the Bayview B and B."

"What?" she shrieked.

Danny reached over and patted her knee. "Relax. It will all make sense."

"If you think, Danny O'Flaherty," she began, her nostrils flaring, "that I'm going to check into a hotel room with you, then you are sadly mistaken."

"Now, Fidelma, it's not what you're thinking. Trust me. Do you know anybody at Bayview?"

"Of course not."

"Good, then you won't be recognized."

"But—"

Danny held up his hand for silence as he found a parking spot a few blocks from the Bed & Breakfast on the off chance that Seamus Larkin would recognize his car if he parked out front.

"You're Mrs. Danny O'Flaherty," he instructed, "over from America for holiday. You don't need to say too much. I'll do the talking."

"I don't like this a-tall."

Danny switched off the ignition and looked over at Fidelma. "Trust me."

To make their story believable, Danny had his suitcase in the boot of the car. He got the suitcase out, took Fidelma by the hand, and walked toward the B&B—a happy Irish-American couple on vacation, exploring the land of their ancestors. Except, Danny noted, Fidelma didn't look happy. She scowled as they walked along the sidewalk. But that's all right, Danny was thinking, the tourists he had seen so far in Ireland usually looked unhappy when he saw them. It would be more convincing this way.

The Bayview was a large, two-story house on O'Connell Street, overlooking the bay. At the foot of the street was a wide, sandy beach. A man was riding a horse swiftly down the beach.

"Ready?" Danny asked, as they opened the door of the porch along the front of the B&B.

Fidelma looked at him crossly and said nothing as they walked through the porch where an elderly couple played cards at a small table. Danny opened the door of the main residence and they went inside.

A middle-aged woman greeted them as Danny showed his passport and signed the guest registry. "Your first time in Ireland, Mr. O'Flaherty?" she asked, looking down at the name in the passport.

"Yes. My wife and I are over for a week seeing

the sights." Danny, obviously enjoying the charade, squeezed Fidelma's hand and looked at her as if they were newlyweds.

Fidelma glared back at him.

"Ah, sure, that's grand," said the landlady. "What part of the States are ye from?"

"New York."

"And you Mrs. O'Flaherty, are you enjoying our country?"

Fidelma looked terror-stricken. Her accent would prove Danny a liar and she glared at him again, obviously hating him for having put them into such a preposterous position. "It's okay," she mumbled in a fake American accent that sounded like a cross between John Wayne and a waitress in a Pittsburgh diner.

"She hasn't been feeling well," Danny continued, fully into the role now. "We've been doing too much sightseeing. I think she's a little tired."

"Oh, where have you been?"

Danny faltered for a moment and he could see Fidelma stiffen beside him. "Uh...Bunratty Castle," he said, frantically ransacking his mind for Irish tourist sights, "Blarney Castle, the lakes of Killary, the Ring of Karney."

Fidelma emitted a short laugh that sounded like a noise from a dying animal.

The landlady held up a finger. "That's the lakes

of Killarney, and the Ring of Kerry,'' she corrected.

''Yeah, well, you know. All that stuff.''

The landlady glanced quickly back at the passport and up at Danny and Fidelma, studying their faces briefly. ''Will you be at Bayview long?''

''No,'' Fidelma hissed vehemently, digging her fingernails into Danny's arm.

''No,'' he echoed, throwing her a dirty look and trying to laugh. ''You see, my wife,'' he searched for words, ''is anxious to get on to see,'' again Danny ransacked his mind for Irish tourist spots, ''the Dingle Peninsula.''

The landlady looked at him oddly. ''So you're going back down to Kerry, sure? But you're spending the night up here?'' She looked quizzically at the couple. ''Sure, why didn't you see Dingle when you were down that way?''

Danny was blundering badly and the game had suddenly lost its appeal. Again he tried to laugh it off. ''Oh, you know, we're on vacation,'' he glanced quickly at Fidelma, who looked stricken. ''We have no planned itinerary. Just wherever we hang our hats,'' Danny trailed off with the cliché, smiling ludicrously.

The landlady looked at him with suspicion as she handed back his passport and scanned the board of keys next to her.

''Would Room Twelve be free by chance?''

Danny asked, trying to sound nonchalant. The landlady looked up at him sharply and furrowed her brow. Danny blundered on, trying to explain. "Our lucky number," he said, looking lovingly at Fidelma, who had murder in her eyes.

"Lucky number?" the landlady parroted, probably thinking that she had a real nut case on her hands.

Danny laughed unconvincingly. "Yeah. Just a little thing we have. Kind of silly, really." He looked to Fidelma for support, but she turned away.

The landlady studied his face for a full moment, then smiled at them. "Ah, you Yanks. Sure, I've never understood your ways. But that's what makes life grand, isn't it?" She took the key to room twelve down and handed it to Danny.

"Yeah," Danny said feebly. "Grand!"

Fidelma was practically drawing blood with her nails buried in his arm.

"Enjoy your stay," the landlady called cheerily as they trudged up the stairs toward their room.

As soon as Danny closed the door, Fidelma turned on him like a rabid dog. "Are you a bleeding idjut?" she screamed.

Danny held his forefinger to his lips, afraid that Seamus Larkin next door would hear. "We've got to keep quiet," he whispered.

"Danny O'Flaherty, this is the most ridiculous caper—"

Danny grimaced and held his hands against Fidelma's lips. "Sssh. He'll hear us."

"Who?"

Danny led Fidelma to a chair and sat her down. He sat on the bed, leaned over and whispered, "Now, listen. Seamus Larkin is in the room next door. He's supposed to meet someone here tonight, who I think is going to cast a great deal of light on this case."

"Do you mean to tell me—" Fidelma started, but Danny held his quivering finger frantically to his lips and waved his other hand for silence. Fidelma lowered her voice to a whisper, "that you've brought me here, checked into a room with me, and now you're asking me to spy on Seamus Larkin, the publican of our village pub, and a respected member of our parish? Is that what you're trying to tell me, Danny O'Flaherty?"

"Well, you make it sound so—"

Just then they heard a rap next door. The bed creaked as someone got up and moved toward the door. "Who is it?" they heard Seamus Larkin call.

"It's me," a woman answered.

"Now wait a minute," Fidelma whispered between clenched teeth. "I have no intention—"

Danny held his finger to his lips as he moved

off the bed and sat on the floor with his ear pressed to the wall.

"You're late," he heard Seamus Larkin say.

"I'm sorry, Seamus, dear. Sure, I'd to press my brother's shirts when he got home."

Larkin said something back that Danny couldn't catch. Fidelma Muldoon sat horrified on the bed, turning her face away as if trying not to hear what was going on next door.

"Now what is it, dear," Danny heard the woman say, "that you're so worried about."

"It's that bleeding Yank, O'Flaherty."

Fidelma cocked her head when she heard Danny's name; her expression seemed to soften a bit.

"He's been asking questions all over the place." Seamus Larkin affected an American accent and mimicked: "Where were you on Saturday between nine and ten? How well did you know Rose Noonan? Where did you go the afternoon of the murder? What side of the bloody fookin' bed did you get out of this morning? He thinks he's fookin' Sherlock Holmes or something."

Danny looked angrily at Fidelma. He didn't like being mocked. Fidelma moved down beside him on the floor, and she too pressed her ear to the wall.

"So who cares if he asks questions?" they heard the woman ask.

Fidelma cupped a hand around Danny's ear and whispered. "That's the Widow Conlon, sure."

Danny held his finger to his lips.

"He knows, I tell you," Larkin said.

"Sure, he knows nothing," the woman assured him.

Danny looked at Fidelma, whose eyes were wide.

"He does, goddammit. I know he does."

"How?"

"Well, he was asking questions around to everyone in the pub. Sure, he asked me what I was doing between nine and ten o'clock on Saturday when Rose was killed. He looked at me suspicious-like, with his little notebook flipped open, taking notes."

"Sure, and what did you tell him?" Widow Conlon asked breathlessly. "You didn't tell him…?"

"Of course not, you silly woman. Do you think I was born yesterday? I told him I was down to Harris Brothers in Kilkee to buy a bit of pipe for the sink at the pub."

The woman seemed relieved. "Well, sure that's a good one. Did he believe you?"

"I thought he did," Seamus Larkin said bitterly. "How was I to know he'd actually go ask Declan Harris was I there on Saturday."

"He did?" Widow Conlon asked in amazement.

"Sure, he goes up and asks Declan had he seen Seamus Larkin. Declan tells him, 'sure, I haven't seen Seamus Larkin in a year.' So he knows."

"But he doesn't know *where* you were," Widow Conlon protested.

"Sure, he'll put two and two together. He's not an idjut. Though he might act like one."

Danny nearly rose from where he sat with his ear pressed against the wall. But he stayed put and shook his fist at Seamus Larkin. Fidelma grabbed his hand and brought it down onto her lap. Her own hands were shaking.

"I'm doomed," he heard Seamus Larkin say heavily. "If he doesn't know now, he'll find it all out soon enough."

Fidelma looked at Danny with hatred in her eyes. Danny nodded his head sagely, then leaned over and whispered, "Didn't I tell you?"

"I can't believe it," Fidelma whispered back. "He and the widow in it together? I didn't even know they knew each other. I mean not like this. You think the two of them planned Rose's murder?"

"I don't know, but she certainly knew about it."

Then they heard Widow Conlon ask Seamus Larkin, "What are you going to do?"

"Sure, I don't know. What can I do?"

Fidelma looked as though she were ready to jump up, break down the door, and strangle

Seamus Larkin to death. "That bloody bastard," she hissed. Then she began to sniffle. "How could he do this?"

"You know I suspected him all along," Danny said, gloating. "Didn't take much to figure out, really." He held Fidelma's hand and waxed philosophical. "You see, it's a simple matter of motive and opportunity."

Danny and Fidelma talked quietly. Danny comforted her as she sniffled, and he explained how he had solved the mystery of Rose's murder. Then they heard the Widow Conlon and Seamus Larkin talking again.

"Sure, you know if Mammy finds out what she'll do?"

Danny looked quizzically at Fidelma, and pressed his ear once again to the wall.

"Oh, Seamus," the widow sighed.

"Sure, she needs me. I sent her money all those years I lived in England. All she ever talked about when she wrote me was the day I'd come back to Ballycara to look after her. You know I was the baby of the family."

"I know, Seamus," the widow said sadly.

"When she finds out, sure won't her poor heart be broken."

To Danny's dismay, Seamus Larkin began to weep.

Fidelma looked at Danny oddly. "What's he talking about?"

Danny shrugged.

"Seamus, darling, you know I understand. But you're a grown man now. You can't be tied to your mammy's apron strings your whole life. You're a big strong man, with desires of the flesh. You're only mortal, for God's sake."

Seamus Larkin was sniffling like a little baby. "But you don't know my mother. If she finds out I've been seeing a woman, God knows, I don't know what she'll do."

Fidelma looked at Danny with the light of understanding beginning to cross her features.

Larkin blubbered on. "If that O'Flaherty character finds out I was here with you last Saturday morning, sure he's likely to spread it all over the place. You know the tongues will be flapping, and it will get back to mother. The poor, dear woman's too old for that sort of thing."

Fidelma Muldoon was looking at Danny with murder in her eyes once again. But the intended victim was no longer Seamus Larkin.

"Don't worry so much," said Widow Conlon.

"But you don't understand the way she is. She wants me home with her. Sure, she even resents the time I spend working in the pub. Doesn't she want me waiting on her hand and foot every blessed moment of the day."

"Ah, Seamus."

"Danny O'Flaherty," Fidelma hissed through her teeth. But they both pressed their ears again to hear Larkin.

"I wish they'd find the bloody bastard who killed Rose Noonan, so that Danny O'Flaherty would be satisfied and go back to his own country where he belongs."

"Sure, they'll find who did it, Seamus," the widow consoled him. "Garda Kelley will bring the blackguard who did it, to justice."

Fidelma rose angrily. She brushed off her skirt with brisk slaps and wheeled around at Danny, who had also risen from the floor and was holding up his hands, trying to calm her. "Danny O'Flaherty," she began quietly. "You brought me up here," she said, her voice rising, "to spy on these two poor innocent people who happen to be in love."

"But Fidelma," Danny began weakly. "I had no idea—"

Fidelma snatched her sweater from the bed and started for the door. "You had no idea. I think you had a good idea. I think," she was nearly shouting now, "that you brought me up here under false pretenses, to see what you could get out of a good Catholic girl. You blackguard!"

Danny noticed that the talking next door had ceased.

Fidelma shouted. "You brought me up here. Checked me into a hotel," Fidelma had angrily ripped open the door of the room and was screaming from the hallway, "and lied to me in the most shameful manner possible. Danny O'Flaherty," she screamed, as she descended the stairs, "I think you're some kind of pervert!"

Danny grabbed his suitcase off the bed and ran after her. He looked back up toward the room long enough to see Seamus Larkin and the Widow Conlon standing in the hall, looking at him quizzically.

"Fidelma!" Danny called as he descended the stairs.

"What have you done to that woman?" the landlady was screaming as Danny ran past the registration desk. "I knew you were a blackguard as soon as I laid eyes on you, what with your lakes of Killary and your Ring of Karney. Do you think we're such *amadáns* in Ireland that we can't spot a blackguard when we see one? I'm calling the *garda* right this moment, and don't you forget I've your passport number and your name."

Danny was in the street running frantically after Fidelma as the landlady ran behind him screaming. "What do you take us for in Ireland? Don't let me ever see your face back in The Bayview!"

Danny had outdistanced the landlady, but Fidelma stopped him in his tracks when she turned and screamed, "I don't ever want to see you again.

Do you hear me!'' She disappeared around a corner.

Danny walked slowly back to his car. He heaved himself behind the wheel and dropped his head into his hands. ''Jesus, Mary, and Joseph,'' he muttered.

# FOURTEEN

DANNY MOPED AROUND Shannonside all the next day as if he were a condemned man. He had never been so depressed in his life. He didn't even want to get out of bed. Lying with his head propped up on the pillow, he looked out the window. The sky was the color of dirty dishwater, and the rain fell steadily against the window pane. The room itself was chilly and damp and Danny pulled the blanket around his neck, shivering. He wanted to go home. He was sick of Ireland. He didn't blame his grandfather for fleeing this dreary little island with its miserable food, bitter black beer, tyrannical priests, repressed, guilt-ridden populace, and more bullshit artists per square mile than anywhere Danny had been in his life. He was even sick of the *craic*. Was that all the Irish could do, he asked himself. Tell tall tales, spin yarns, pile one story on top of another on top of another in order to conceal from themselves and everyone else, for that matter, that Ireland was nowhere? And always would be.

Danny sighed and turned from the window. How could things have gone so wrong, so quickly? He'd only been in the country for a week, and as things stood, the person he came to visit had been murdered, he was a chief suspect in the crime, he had fallen in love (was he admitting that to himself now?) and the object of his affection swore she never wanted to see him again. Why in God's name did he ever come here?

He threw the covers off and moved to the window. The rain stood in puddles in the street; the village was silent as a corpse.

He dressed slowly in his freshest clothes, looped a tie around his neck and knotted it carefully. He wasn't going anywhere, but somehow dressing up made him feel better.

Danny got out pencil and paper and spent the morning working on his family tree. It looked something like this:

*Daniel O'Flaherty & Mary Galvin O'Flaherty*

⬇

*Daniel P. (I) & Maureen (Duffey) & Sean*

⬇　　　　　　　⬇　　　　　　　⬇

*Daniel P. (II) Johnny & Michael   Rose (Noonan)*

⬇　　　　　　　　　　　　　　　⬇

*Daniel P. (III)　　　　　　　Mona Noonan*

Now that he had written it down, it seemed clearer than ever. Although he understood his relationship to these people, somehow it had been cloudy in his mind. What amazed him was how many people in the village understood the genealogy of his family so clearly. The older ones, like Mrs. Slattery, rattled off names and dates as if she were talking about her own family. Perhaps the pace of life allowed them to think about genealogy more. But that seemed like too simple an explanation. Perhaps, Danny thought bitterly, it was that the Irish were so damned interested in everyone else's business.

Somehow, the process of making the chart eased Danny's mind, although one thing that still puzzled him was the origin of the ''P'' in his grandfather's name.

He felt slightly better, though still embarrassed by the disaster of the night before. He went down to breakfast.

''Sure, you look like you're after coming from Mass,'' said Mrs. Slattery as he sat down to breakfast.

''Oh,'' Danny fingered the tie. He'd forgotten about putting it on. He smiled self-consciously. ''Just a change of pace.''

''Sure, it's grand,'' she said, pouring him a cup of tea. ''Where are you off to?''

Danny shook his head thoughtfully. ''Nowhere. Not today.'' He jerked his head toward the door. ''Too nasty out.''

''That it is.''

"I think I'll just stay here and rest today. It's been a hard," Danny hesitated, "couple of days."

"Sure, just relax. 'Tis a soft day. I'll fix us a bit of fish for tea. Maybe you can run over to the pub for a few pints in the evening. Take your mind off t'ings."

Danny cringed. The thought of going over to Larkin's Pub horrified him. How would he explain to Seamus Larkin what he was doing at Bayview last night? He could see that bastard's face now, all screwed up and smirking. He could even hear the publican's obscene voice: *After having a bit of a roll in the hay with Fidelma Muldoon, are ye?* The pig.

But wait a minute, Danny thought suddenly. Haven't I got something on him? Wasn't he blubbering up there like a little baby, afraid his mommy would find out that he had a girlfriend? How repressed can you get? Seamus Larkin must be fifty years old and still wheedling for his mother's approval.

"Yes," Danny said to Mrs. Slattery. "Maybe I will go over for a few pints this evening."

"That's right. You'll feel better, sure. Peadar MacGreevy tells me you're quite the star over there."

"Oh, really?"

"Sure, he says they're always talking about the Yank whenever you're not there."

"I'll bet," said Danny absently. "When were you talking to Peadar MacGreevy?"

"Ah, he was over last Sunday after Mass for a visit when you were down with Fidelma, looking at the parish records. Sure, the lads in the pub think the world of you, Danny."

That made Danny feel better. The Irish might have their problems, he reasoned, but at least they were good judges of character.

After breakfast, Danny went back up to his room. He spent the rest of the morning making another chart with the names of potential suspects, and a list of possible motivations for Rose's murder. Why do people kill each other? Greed, revenge, jealousy, lust, pride? The list seemed somehow inadequate.

Danny put his pencil down and thought of Fidelma. How could he have botched that so badly? She was a beautiful woman, kind and thoughtful, and such a lovely brogue. Danny ended up looking like some kind of a lecherous... What had she called him? Pervert!

She said she never wanted to see him again. Of all the people in the village, he had gotten the closest to Fidelma. Now she hated him. Why? Well, she had a right to, Danny supposed. After all, that had been a pretty bizarre scene at Bayview last night. Danny chuckled in spite of himself.

Danny took out his chart of the family tree again

and stared at it. He still had a nagging suspicion that Rose was going to tell him some secret about his grandfather before she was murdered. Danny was also convinced that someone didn't want him to know that information, and that was why Rose had been killed. It was the only hunch he had to go on now that the trail to Seamus Larkin had led to a dead end. He had to follow it up.

But what could that information possibly be? Whoever had taken the letter from his room must have thought that Rose had disclosed something in her letter. Had she? He didn't even have the letter to read again.

Danny fell back on the bed with a sigh. He wished he could just forget about this whole thing, grab the next plane out of Shannon, and get back to the States. But it was doubtful he could even leave the country. As far as he knew, he was still a suspect in the crime.

Then something popped suddenly into Danny's mind: the photograph he had seen at Rose's house yesterday after the burial—the photo of his great-grandmother with a baby in her arms. The caption under the photo read: "Our first-born. Sean Michael O'Flaherty, 1893."

Danny sat up on the bed and reached for his family tree. The caption had struck Danny as odd when he'd first read it. Our first-born? But wasn't Daniel P. O'Flaherty the first born? Danny flipped through his notes and papers regarding his genealogical research, and pulled out the certified copy of his grandfather's birth certificate. It read: "Daniel P. O'Flaherty. Born: July 16, 1890."

Danny sat puzzling over the discovery. Clearly, his grandfather had been born three years before his brother Sean (Rose's father). Yet the inscription on the back of the photograph had said, "our first born." Was that just a mistake on the part of the person who had written it? How could it be? No woman could possibly mistake the order in which her children were born. And whoever had written it had stated emphatically: "Our first-born. Sean Michael O'Flaherty, 1893."

Danny flipped back through his notes for any other information that might throw some light on this. If he was the first-born, the date on the photograph had to be wrong. He could not possibly have been born in 1893 and be the first-born. Daniel P. O'Flaherty's birth certificate legally established his date of birth as 1890. Sean would have to have been born before 1890. Perhaps a check of Sean's birth certificate at Births, Deaths, & Marriages would clarify the discrepancy. Danny made a note to do just that.

But in the meantime, what did it mean? So what if Danny had thought that his grandfather was the first-born of the three? As it turned out, perhaps Rose's father was the first-born. What did it mean?

Danny got up and paced. For one thing, it would explain why his grandfather had emigrated. If he had been the first-born he would have come into the farm, as they said. He would have inherited the farm, stayed in Ireland, and Sean would have emigrated. Maureen O'Flaherty had married Dermott Duffey, and in that sense came into the Duffey farm that Johnny and Mickey had in turn inherited.

So maybe what Rose had intended to tell Danny was that, contrary to family history, his grandfather had not been the first born of the O'Flaherty family. But that was hardly earth-shattering, was it? What would that have to do with Rose's murder?

Danny scanned back through his notes, trying to turn up something that might answer the question. But he gave up in frustration, fell back on the bed, and slept the afternoon away.

Danny woke up to the sound of someone shouting his name. "Danny, Danny!"

It was Mrs. Slattery.

He got up feeling dopey, and looked around. The rain still persisted outside, and he was glad that he had stayed in all day. No need to go out in that mess.

Downstairs, Mrs. Slattery brought in a steaming pot of boiled potatoes from the kitchen, a filet of poached salmon smothered with mushrooms, and a plate of boiled carrots.

"Bless us O Lord," she began, "and these Thy

gifts, which we are about to receive from Thy bounty, through Christ, Our Lord. Amen.''

Danny blessed himself and took up his fork. Irish food wasn't so bad, he was thinking. It was simple, wholesome, and in Mrs. Slattery's home, delicious. It was those awful fish-and-chips take-aways that Danny had sampled in Kilkee and Ennis that were unbearable.

After eating, Danny crossed the rainy street to Larkin's Pub. The hubbub died suddenly as he walked in, and Danny felt the way he had the first time he had come to Larkin's—a stranger.

As usual, Seamus Larkin was behind the bar. Liam Flynn and Tim Mahoney were at their places in front of the fire. Peadar MacGreevy sat rolling a cigarette and talking to Brendan Grady at the bar. All eyes were on Danny.

''Pint of Harp,'' he said to Seamus Larkin, who was looking at him with a smile on his face—the only time Danny had ever seen him smile.

Danny sat down and put a ten-pound note (the one with Jonathan Swift on it) on the bar.

Larkin set his Harp in front of him and picked up the note. Still no one had spoken.

''Back from Kilkee so soon?'' Larkin finally broke the silence, sneering sarcastically.

''Yeah,'' Danny countered. ''And you?''

Larkin moved to the other end of the bar and the rest of the patrons turned back to their pints and resumed their conversations. Danny stared down into his pint. He felt more alone than he had since arriving in Ireland, and he missed Fidelma. Would she ever speak to him again?

"I suppose you've heard the news, Danny," Tim Mahoney called to him from across the room.

Danny swung around, grateful that someone had finally addressed him. "What's that?"

"They've charged Paddy Carmody with robbery. Apparently they believe his story about Rose being dead when he got there. No murder charges."

Danny looked at Tim. "I believe him, too."

"'Tis a queer caper," said Peadar MacGreevy.

"Sure, the whole thing's been queer," agreed Brendan Grady. "That damn fool Kelley is no closer to figuring this thing out than the day Rose died. Sure, and he's keeping poor Danny here not knowing what to do next."

"When are you supposed to go home, Danny?" Tim asked.

"I'm *supposed* to go home the day after tomorrow. I suppose I better see about changing those plans."

"Looks as though you might have to," Seamus Larkin said acidly.

Danny took another long drink of his pint and sighed.

"Something troubling you?" Seamus Larkin asked sarcastically.

"No, everything's grand," Danny said, barely able to suppress his anger. "My cousin's been murdered, and I'm accused of it. I'm supposed to fly home in two days, and I don't know when I'll be able to leave. Fidelma Muldoon says—" Danny stopped suddenly and looked up. Larkin was grinning like an idiot. "Everything's just grand," Danny grumbled, "grand."

"Ah, don't worry about it," said Larkin, putting the knife in and twisting. "I'm sure Donal Kelley will crack the case within the year."

The whole pub burst into guffaws.

Danny sat simmering and sipped his pint. He should have stayed back at Shannonside. Why did he come over here?

"Sure, he's just codding you," said Peadar MacGreevy, taking pity on Danny.

"About all I've heard since I've gotten to Ireland," Danny said bitterly, "is a bunch of cod."

Everyone in the pub laughed. Danny's frustration seemed to peak, and all at once he was laughing, too. A week ago he would not even have known what they meant by "cod." Bullshit is what he would have called it. And now he was laughing with everyone in the pub...at himself.

Danny drained his glass and called for a round for everyone. "Fill 'em up, Seamus. The night is young." No wonder he was so popular at Larkin's Pub, Danny thought bitterly, as he reached for his wallet. He was always buying them rounds. And you never heard a complaint out of anyone.

Larkin drew the pints of Guinness with care, leaving them to settle on the drain board.

"Give me a Guinness this time," Danny amended, feeling adventurous.

"Sure, you want some of the real stuff?" Larkin asked condescendingly.

"Yeah. The real stuff."

Seamus Larkin handed out the stouts and everyone in the pub, Tim Mahoney, Brendan Grady, Peadar MacGreevy, and Liam Flynn gathered around Danny for a toast.

*"Sláinte,"* they chorused, then buried their faces in the mouths of their jars.

Danny took a long drink of his stout, wiped the cream off his mustache with the back of his hand, and smacked his lips.

"I'm off to the loo, lads," he said, standing up and heading to the back of the pub.

I've got to stop talking like this, he said to himself as he walked back to the bathroom. They'll think I'm flakey back in New York. Danny fumbled with his zipper in the bathroom and let out a spray of urine. *If* I ever get back to New York, he thought with a shudder.

When he got back to the bar Brendan Grady had begun a song: "Wearing of the Green."

Danny sipped on his stout and listened as the rest of the men joined in the song. The stout was more bitter than he remembered. He looked into his jar. He was sure now that he preferred the Harp.

Suddenly Danny felt sleepy. Brendan Grady and Tim Mahoney had launched into another song, but Danny was too tired to listen. He got up unsteadily, tipping over the last of his stout as he turned. He reached for the glass as it rolled off the bar, missed it, and watched it shatter on the floor.

"Sorry," he said thickly, staring down at the shards of glass glittering in the brown pool of stout.

Seamus Larkin came angrily from behind the bar with a mop in his hand. The singing came to a chaotic halt as all eyes turned on Danny.

"I'm off, lads," he said, his voice sounding oddly distant, even alien.

"So soon?" someone called.

"A bit too much of the drink taken," snapped Seamus Larkin, as he cleaned up the mess with angry strokes of the mop. "Can't handle the good stuff."

Danny stumbled out the door.

Outside, the cold, damp air slapped him in the face and he steadied himself against the side of the pub. I only had two pints, he was thinking, as he lurched across the road toward Shannonside. His legs felt weak and a numbness settled across his face. Suddenly he felt a gut-wrenching pain in his abdomen and he doubled over in agony. Forcing himself to straighten up, he leaned heavily against the door of Mrs. Slattery's house, and pounded on it with a weak hand. He could barely hear the footsteps, inside, coming toward the door.

Now the sky was spinning violently and he steadied himself against the door. What in God's name is wrong with me? Danny wondered, then he leaned over and vomited into the rose bushes.

When Mrs. Slattery opened the door, he passed out in her arms.

# FIFTEEN

"WHERE AM I?" Danny asked.

Mrs. Slattery hovered over his bed, where he lay soaking in sweat.

"Praise be to God," the old woman blessed herself. "You're alive."

Danny looked around the room. He had an exploding headache and a burning in the pit of his stomach. He looked at the picture of St. Martin on the wall and then into Mrs. Slattery's worried eyes. "What time is it?"

Mrs. Slattery put a cold, damp washcloth on his forehead. "The doctor's after leaving. You've been sleeping for nearly twenty hours."

"The doctor?" Danny mumbled.

"Sure, we didn't know if you'd wake up a-tall."

Danny drifted in and out of sleep. "What happened?" he managed to ask.

"Sure, wouldn't we all like to know. Doctor Cassidy is analyzing the stuff he pumped out of your stomach last night. He said he'd let us know as soon as he learned anything."

"My stomach?"

"In the meantime, you're to rest easy, sure."

Danny lay back on the pillow, his head throbbing. He drifted in and out of consciousness. His face and limbs felt numb and he flip-flopped between chills and fever. He fell again into a deep sleep.

When he woke up, an elderly man with a stethoscope around his neck, gazed down on him.

"How are you feeling?" the doctor prompted.

Danny could barely open his mouth to answer. His vision was blurry and the doctor's face wavered in and out of his sight. "Tired," Danny finally managed.

Mrs. Slattery stood in back of the room looking on anxiously.

"Well," the doctor said, "we've found traces of arsenic in your bile and urine."

"Arsenic," Danny murmured.

"That's correct." The doctor looked away from Danny, as if what he was about to say was distasteful to him. "It seems that someone tried to poison you."

"Poison?"

"Does he understand what you're saying a-tall?" Mrs. Slattery asked, as if Danny were not even there.

"Sure, he does."

Danny nodded in agreement.

"We pumped most of it out last night. It was

quite a heavy dosage, but I believe you're going to be all right.''

The doctor gave Danny's arm a squeeze. ''Mrs. Slattery here will be looking out for you. You're on the mend now, sure. But don't hesitate to ring me up if you feel any worse.''

Danny was fully awake now. ''Thank you, doctor.''

Mrs. Slattery came into his vision, wringing her hands.

Was it the food? Danny wondered. He looked at Doctor Cassidy as he prepared to leave. He tried to reach out and grab the doctor so that he would not leave him alone in the house, but he was too weak to move his arm. Had Mrs. Slattery tried to kill him?

''Thank you, Dr. Cassidy,'' he heard her say. ''Sure, I'll be taking good care of him, I can assure you of that.''

''I know you will,'' the doctor said.

Didn't she serve him mushrooms? Maybe she gave him poison mushrooms. But the doctor said arsenic. Then Danny remembered going to the pub. He had ordered a pint of stout. Everyone in the pub had gathered 'round for a toast: Seamus Larkin, Liam Flynn, Brendan Grady, Peadar Mac-Greevy and Tim Mahoney. He'd then excused himself to use the bathroom. While he was gone someone must have put arsenic into his stout.

Thank God he hadn't been able to finish the pint; he'd spilled nearly half of it when he'd tipped over his jar. Had he drunk the whole thing he might be dead by now.

Danny drifted back to sleep, then woke later after the sun had gone down. So, now he had narrowed the suspects to five. Four really: Liam Flynn, Brendan Grady, Peadar MacGreevy, and Tim Mahoney. He was sure Seamus Larkin had nothing to do with Rose's death. But one of those four had surely put something in his stout to kill him.

Danny wiped the perspiration from his forehead and lay there in the dark, thinking. One of those four had to be responsible for Rose's murder. One of those four had broken into his room and taken the letter from him. One of those four had poisoned his stout. And one of those four knew something about his grandfather that he didn't want Danny to know.

Danny tried to remember the exact location of each one of them as they had toasted him, and to remember which one could have put something in his stout when he went to the bathroom. As he recalled, any one of them could have done it.

Danny drifted back to sleep and in the morning was awakened by a knock on the door. He looked weakly around the room. The rain had ceased and a welcome ray of sunlight shone through the window of the bedroom. "Who is it?" he called softly.

"You've a visitor," Mrs. Slattery answered.

The door opened and Fidelma Muldoon stood framed by the doorway. Danny turned his head on the pillow for a better look and smiled.

The smile triggered something in Fidelma and she dashed across the room and gave him a hug. "Oh, Danny. Sure, I'm just after hearing what happened t'you. I'm so sorry about the other night. I know it wasn't your fault. You were just trying to catch the murderer."

Danny stroked her long hair. "I was afraid I'd never see you again."

Fidelma sat up on the bed and looked into Danny's eyes. "Do you forgive me?"

"Do you forgive me?" Danny countered.

"Of course I do. I'm sorry I got so angry with you, Danny."

"It's okay."

"Who did this to you?"

Danny sat up painfully, and propped a pillow behind his head. "One of four people. Either Liam Flynn, Tim Mahoney, Peadar MacGreevy, or Brendan Grady."

"It happened at the pub?"

"Yeah."

"What about Seamus Larkin? He was there."

"You heard him the other night, Fidelma. I

don't think he knows anything about who killed Rose.''

"That's true," admitted Fidelma. "You're sure this has something to do with Rose's death?''

"Positive. Someone thinks I know more than I do," said Danny.

"What are you going to do?''

"Well, I have an idea that Rose was going to tell me something about my grandfather that someone didn't want me to know. I don't know what she was going to tell me, or why someone doesn't want me to know it. But I have a hunch. And I'm certain it's linked to everything that has happened.''

Fidelma looked at him with a worried expression. "What is it, Danny?''

"I'm convinced now that my grandfather was not the first-born child of Daniel and Mary O'Flaherty. Rose's father was their first-born.''

"But your grandfather was older than Sean Michael.''

"Older, yes. But not necessarily their first-born.''

Fidelma looked at him. "And what has that to do with the murder of Rose?''

"I'm not sure, exactly. But I have a good idea. I just need more information.''

"How can I help?" Fidelma asked, without any visible enthusiasm.

"I want you to go back to the parish registry and check the baptismal records of these people." Danny handed her the list he had drawn up. Liam Flynn, Tim Mahoney, Peadar MacGreevy, Brendan Grady, Sean Michael O'Flaherty, Maureen O'Flaherty Duffey. "I want you to go back in the record as far as you can. Look up the date that each of these were baptized, and their parents, and their parents' parents, if possible. As far back as the record goes."

"What do you expect to find?"

"I'm not sure yet. When I see all the dates, I'm hoping something is going to fall into place that will pinpoint one of these four."

Fidelma folded the list and put it in her purse.

"In the meantime," Danny continued, painfully trying to rise up out of the bed, "I've got a few more questions to ask. And I've got to go back to Births, Deaths, and Marriages in Ennis. There's one more family tree I need to shake."

"Oh no you don't," said Fidelma, pushing him back against the pillow.

Danny submitted momentarily, then gathered his strength and rose despite Fidelma's protests. He pulled the blanket around his waist to cover himself, hobbled over to the wardrobe, and took out a pair of pants.

"What are you doing?" she asked.

"I'm going to Ennis."

"But Danny, you're too sick. You need to stay in bed."

Danny pulled his pants off the wooden hanger and let the blanket fall from around his waist. As Fidelma turned her back on him, Danny pulled the pants on in a flash.

"Now," he said, feeling much better as he grabbed a shirt and jacket, "I'm off to Ennis."

"But Danny..."

"No buts about it. I'm supposed to be on a plane leaving Shannon tonight. I want to be on that plane."

"You don't like Ireland?"

"Fidelma! I've got to get to the bottom of this crime. I'm sure I'm close to solving this thing. When I do, I'm going home. Is that so hard for you to understand?"

Fidelma smiled. "Of course not."

"Now, I should be back from Ennis by late afternoon. When do you think you can look up those records?"

"Sure, I'll do it right now. Father O'Malley is in Dublin for some kind of retreat. I've got nothing but time on me hands."

"I have one other favor to ask."

"Sure."

"I want you to tell everyone in the village to come to Larkin's Pub today at," Danny glanced at his watch, "two o'clock. That will give me five hours to go to Ennis, look up the information I need, and get back. Will that give you enough time?''

"Yes. But why do you want everyone at the pub?''

"By the time I get back from Ennis I'm sure I'll know who murdered Rose and I plan to announce it to the whole village, including that thick-headed Garda Kelley.''

Fidelma looked doubtful. "This isn't going to be another one of your capers like Bayview, I hope.''

Danny took her hands in his and looked at her. "Trust me.''

"That's what you said last time.''

"Will you just make sure everyone's at the pub at two o'clock, please?''

"All right.''

"Good," Danny said, picking up his notes. He put on his jacket and started out the door. "You need a ride down to the rectory?'' Danny asked.

"No. I'll walk.''

"Are you sure?''

"Yes.''

Danny grabbed the family tree he had made and started to show it to Fidelma, but changed his mind and put it in his coat pocket. "OK. See you at two o'clock at Larkin's.''

"Good luck," said Fidelma.

# SIXTEEN

AT TWO O'CLOCK that afternoon at Larkin's Pub, Danny O'Flaherty took a sip of his Harp and arranged his notes and exhibits on the small table in front of him like a well-trained solicitor. Spread before him were the photocopies from Births, Deaths & Marriages he had made that morning in Ennis, the family tree chart he had made earlier, the photograph of his grandfather, and various other bits of evidence that he intended to present.

Fidelma rushed in with the baptismal records and handed them to him. Danny glanced at them cursorily. "Good. Thanks," he said, and placed them in front of him on the table.

He took another sip of Harp, cleared his throat, and addressed the group. "I've asked all of you to come here today because I have a plane to catch at six o'clock." He glanced at his watch. "Four hours from now." Danny looked over at Garda Kelley. "And I intend to be on that plane."

Kelley raised his bushy eyebrows as if to say, "We'll see about that."

"I came to Ireland to find out who I am," began Danny. "A lot of unexpected things have happened since I got here. Most unbelievable, of course, was the brutal and senseless murder of Rose O'Flaherty Noonan.'' Danny paused. ''I began to realize that if I were to discover who the murderer of Rose Noonan was, I first had to discover who I am. And so in order to explain to you, I need to tell a story. First of all, I need to tell you who I am. My name is Daniel P. O'Flaherty, the Third.''

Danny overheard Garda Kelley say to the fellow next to him, ''Sure, isn't he brilliant. He knows his own name.''

Danny held up a hand for silence and continued. ''My grandfather was Daniel P. O'Flaherty, the First. Some of you knew him personally. He was born in eighteen ninety and he died at the age of seventy, in nineteen sixty. According to the baptismal record of St. Bridget's Catholic Church, in the Parish of Ballycara,'' Danny held up a copy of the record and handed it to Tim Mahoney to pass around the room, ''my grandfather was baptized on May first, eighteen ninety-one. Ten months from the date of his birth.''

Danny gave a meaningful pause for the information to sink in. ''He was the eldest of three children of Mary Galvin O'Flaherty and Daniel O'Flaherty. The 'P' in my grandfather's name, which no one has been able to explain, was given to him at his baptism. I never wondered what this

'P' stood for until I noticed at my great-grandfather's grave that *he* was named, simply, Daniel O'Flaherty. I will explain all of this later.

"Daniel P. O'Flaherty was the oldest," Danny repeated. "The next oldest was Sean Michael O'Flaherty, and the youngest was Maureen O'Flaherty.

"Daniel P. O'Flaherty left Ireland in nineteen nineteen at the age of twenty-eight. A curious thing that the eldest son would leave his inheritance behind and go off to the New World. I puzzled over that one myself for some time."

Brendan Grady hollered from the back of the pub. "Sure, he wasn't exactly leaving Dublin Castle!"

Several people laughed.

"You're right, Brendan," Danny continued. "It was not a great farm, but for those times it was something." Danny paused and looked around at the faces turned up to him in the pub. "Sean and his wife," he continued, "had one child, whom they named Rose. And Rose married James Noonan and they had one child, whom they named Mona." Danny looked over at Mona Noonan, who sat twirling her drink absently, looking into the glass. "The youngest, Maureen, married her childhood sweetheart, Dermott Duffey and they had a set of twins, the lovable Johnny and Mickey Duffey." Johnny and Mickey smiled broadly. "When my great-grandparents, Mary and Daniel O'Flaherty, died, my grandfather, Daniel P. O'Flaherty had already emigrated to the States and Sean O'Flaherty, the next eldest, came into the farm.''

"Oh Christ!" Seamus Larkin called from behind the bar, "We know your family history. Would you get on with it.''

Again, Danny held up his hands for silence. "I'm trying to create a context by which all of you can understand the tragedy that has taken place in our…" Danny corrected himself, "*your* village.

"So far, none of this is particularly remarkable," Danny continued. "Perhaps a typical story of emigration. A story that you have heard thousands of times before. But again, I wish to emphasize three points that *are* remarkable. First," Danny bent his forefinger away from the rest of his hand, "my grandfather was born on July sixteenth, eighteen ninety, but was not baptized until May first, eighteen ninety-one, some ten months later. This seems unusual for a Catholic family in those times. Mrs. Slattery has told me that some families who lived in remote areas often waited until the spring to make the trip down the mountain to the parish church to have the child baptized. But my grandfather was not born in a remote area. Mrs. Slattery has also told me of the graveyards that are beside old churchyards in every part of Ireland.

These were the graveyards of unbaptized children; children who died without the sacrament of baptism were not permitted to be buried in the same graveyard with the baptized, because, as we all know, those poor unbaptized children were relegated to the nether-world of Limbo in the afterlife.''

Danny reached down and took a sip of his Harp. ''Again, I ask you. Why would a good Catholic family, who lived relatively close to the church, risk the soul of their newborn child by waiting almost a year for him to receive the sacrament of baptism?''

''Sure, they were queer times,'' said Liam Flynn angrily. ''How can we know what they were thinking then? The Penal Laws made people afraid to practice their faith.''

''The Penal Laws,'' Danny countered, ''had been relaxed since the early eighteen hundreds.''

Liam Flynn grumbled and sat back in his seat.

''The second fact,'' Danny continued, ticking another finger from his left hand, ''was the curious reversal of a time-honored Irish custom. As we all know, the first-born always inherited all of the land of the family farm. There are some who contend that this custom is partially responsible for the massive emigration from Ireland. Perhaps, if the land had been divided among all the siblings, more people could have stayed in Ireland. As it is, however, all but the eldest were forced to emigrate. Unless they were females who might marry someone else who had inherited a farm. That also explains why many of you men are much older when you marry than we in America. You must wait until both your parents have died before you have the farm that might attract a woman. But I'm digressing.''

''Indeed!'' muttered Seamus Larkin.

Danny regathered his thoughts, trying to weave together all the threads of evidence that had been unraveling since Rose's murder. ''But my grandfather was the oldest in his family. Yet he chose to emigrate, and Sean Michael inherited the farm.''

Mona Noonan spoke for the first time. ''Sure, if you think your grandda was cheated out of the farm, I'll give you the damn thing right now, and good riddance to it.''

The pub burst into a round of appreciative laughter.

Danny struggled to keep focused on his explanation. ''Bear with me. Follow my line of reasoning,'' he implored, then added in hasty annoyance, ''though I know how alien logic is to you Irish.''

''Watch out, man,'' Brendan Grady called goodnaturedly.

''Thirdly,'' Danny continued, raising his three fingers above his head. ''The unexplained 'P' that was added to Grandfather's name. What did it stand for? My examination of the records reveals no Patrick or Paul or Peter or anything else of the sort in our family. Yet this letter was affixed to his name at his baptism.''

Danny looked around the room before continuing. ''To take my second point first, I wondered for days why the oldest person in the family would emigrate and the second oldest would inherit the farm. Then, when I was at the Noonan house after Rose's funeral, I spotted this photograph on the wall. Mona has kindly allowed me to borrow it for this presentation.''

Danny held up the photograph of Rose's grandmother, Mary O'Flaherty, with a small baby in her arms. Danny turned the photograph over. ''I will pass this around for you to examine. On the back of the photograph you will find written: 'Our first-born. Sean Michael O'Flaherty, eighteen ninety-three.'''

Danny looked up as the pub buzzed with chatter. ''This would explain,'' he continued, ''why Sean inherited the land. It would not explain, however, how Sean Michael could be the first-born, when my grandfather, according to the official records, was born on July sixteenth, eighteen ninety and Sean Michael was born in eighteen ninety-three.''

Danny took another sip of his Harp and added, ''I shall explain in due course.''

He handed down the photograph and watched as

it was passed around, turned over, and whispered about.

"As for my first point," he said. "Why would a good, Catholic family of the nineteenth century allow ten months to elapse before baptizing their child?" Danny moved from behind the table and walked toward Mona Noonan. "I've puzzled over that question for some time, as well. Maybe they had simply been too busy with the crops, with calving, with the responsibilities of parenthood."

Danny looked at Mona, then moved on and stood in front of Liam Flynn. "But that seems unlikely, wouldn't you say, Liam?"

Flynn looked momentarily startled, then spat out. "It's ridiculous. The Church came first in the eyes of our ancestors. Sure, even the duties of the farm were secondary to the duties toward saving a child's soul."

Danny nodded in agreement and walked on. "Yes, of course, ridiculous." He turned and eyed Seamus Larkin. "Then, perhaps they had been too lazy, or not as devoted to the Church as we might expect."

Mona Noonan spoke up. "They were not lazy, I can assure you. The lazy would have starved to death in those times. And I know from what my mother told me about them that they were more devoted to the Church than most of us sitting here right now."

"I hear that," shouted Larkin.

Danny moved back behind his table and shuffled the documents in front of him. He picked up another framed photograph and held it up for all to see. "This," he said, "is a picture of the O'Flaherty family." He pointed to each member. "Daniel, Mary, and their children, Sean Michael, Maureen, and my grandfather, Daniel P." He turned the photograph over. "If you read the inscription on the back, you will see that it was written by Rose O'Flaherty Noonan." He held it up so that Mona could see it. "Is this your mother's handwriting, Mona?"

"'Tis," she answered curtly.

"Notice if you will, how Rose refers to the members of her family." Danny read aloud the inscription on the back: "'Grandma & Grandpa O'Flaherty, My father, Sean O'Flaherty, My Aunt Maureen O'Flaherty,'" Danny looked up to see that he had the full attention of the pub, "and finally, 'Daniel P.'"

Danny held up a finger. "Notice that she does not write 'my Uncle Daniel' or, as with the others, 'my Uncle Daniel P. O'Flaherty.' She writes simply, 'Daniel P.'" Danny set the picture down. "I find this odd."

"Come on man, get to the point," said Garda Kelly, annoyed, but curious.

"The point," said Danny, "is that it is also possible that the O'Flahertys waited ten months to have their baby baptized because they did not get the baby until ten months after he was born.''

''What?'' Mona shouted indignantly.

Danny held up his hands for patience. ''It is possible that little Daniel P. was not born to the O'Flahertys, but was born in another house, a Protestant house, and adopted by the O'Flahertys ten months later. And would that not further explain why Mary O'Flaherty called Sean Michael their 'first-born,' because in fact he was their first-born, although Daniel P. was older?''

''Sure, you've got the cart pulling the donkey,'' said Garda Kelley. ''Have you a bit of proof of all this malarkey?''

The pub buzzed with conversation as Danny drained his Harp and motioned to Seamus Larkin for another. He rubbed his temples with the tips of his fingers, the strain of the past several days obviously showing on his face.

Larkin placed the fresh pint of lager in front of him and Danny took a tentative sip, then looked straight at Garda Kelley. ''Let's consider a few other details,'' said Danny, putting the jar of lager down. ''When Rose Noonan wrote to me in the United States, she said that she had something interesting to tell me about my grandfather.'' Danny looked around, scrutinizing the expression on each person's face. ''I'm convinced that someone sitting here in this pub knew what that interesting information was; I am also convinced that he or she knew that Rose was going to tell me that information. This person murdered Rose so that she would not talk, yet the murderer was not sure how much I already knew.

"On Sunday, the murderer broke into my room at Shannonside and found the letter that Rose had written me. The letter only stated that she had something interesting to disclose—it did not say what. Still unsure about how much I knew, that same person put arsenic in my stout in an attempt to shut me up."

Danny moved from behind the table again. He held up a copy of a birth record he had photocopied that morning at Births, Deaths & Marriages in Ennis.

"I have in my hands," he began, "a copy of the birth certificate of a child born on exactly the same day as my grandfather—July sixteenth, eighteen ninety. This child was born into a distinguished Protestant family, in a large home, with all of the comforts that generations of wealth would have provided him in the nineteenth century."

Danny held a second document aloft. "But this child would never enjoy the comforts of that home, nor the love of his parents. Because, as you will see," and Danny shook open the document, "according to this marriage certificate, the parents of this child were married on December fourth, eighteen ninety—nearly five months *after* the birth of their first child.''

Mona Noonan whimpered audibly and looked away from Danny. The pub was silent.

"This would never do," Danny said with a note of bitterness in his voice. "A family of this stature could never raise an illegitimate child in their home. Nor could they contemplate leaving the family fortune to a child born out of wedlock— even though this child would be the rightful heir to the estate.''

Danny paused, took a deep breath, sipped his Harp, and steeled his nerves for the final disclosure. "This poor child was given away sometime between the day of his birth and the time of his parents' marriage, to be raised in the home of the poor Catholic couple who lived on the border of the estate. He would never know his true parents, but would enjoy the love and affection of his adopted ones. He would never know the wealth of his true parents, nor would he enter the door of the manor house to which he was rightful heir as anything but a servant. Indeed, he would never know his true identity. It would take his grandson, a generation later, to solve the mystery of his birth.''

Danny looked into the eyes of Garda Kelley. "This little child, of course, was my grandfather, Daniel P. O'Flaherty.''

Again the pub buzzed with chatter.

"Someone in this room knew the true story of my grandfather's birth," Danny began again. "Someone in this room knew that he had been stripped of his birthright. Someone knew that my grandfather's oldest son was my father, and that I am my father's oldest son. Someone mistakenly believed that I, the eldest son of the eldest son of Daniel P. was here to claim, by primogeniture, the lands and stock and house that was the rightful inheritance of Daniel P."

"What is all this malarkey?" cried Seamus Larkin.

"Lot of cod," Danny heard someone say.

"Garda Kelley," Danny said, handing the documents to him. "Perhaps you can conclude from these why a 'P' was added to my grandfather's name. It is the only thing he ever got from his true parents."

Garda Kelley took the papers awkwardly and adjusted his glasses. He inspected the certificates for a moment then looked up in astonishment. "There was a child," he said in an uncertain voice, "born on July sixteenth, eighteen ninety." He looked around nervously, then back at Danny who stood with his arms folded across his chest.

Danny was enjoying the garda's discomfort. This idiot had put his freedom in jeopardy.

Garda Kelley looked around the room and then back at the papers as if he wanted to bolt.

"Well, speak up," shouted Brendan Grady. "Who were the child's parents?"

Garda Kelly looked at Danny again, a shadow of pain crossing his face. His Adam's apple bobbed as he swallowed deeply. "There was a child born on July sixteenth, eighteen ninety," he repeated, "to Jeremiah Pinkerton the Third, and Lydia Edwards."

Garda Kelly looked at George Pinkerton, who had raised up stiffly in his chair. "Those are your grandparents, aren't they, Mr. Pinkerton?"

# SEVENTEEN

"THIS IS OUTRAGEOUS," cried George Pinkerton.

The pub had burst into noisy argument. George Pinkerton rose, knocking his chair over as he did. The sound of clattering glasses and harsh voices sent dull shocks of pain through Danny's head.

"This is an absolute outrage," George Pinkerton shouted indignantly.

Garda Kelley, still holding the papers, pulled himself upright and took command of the situation. "I'll handle this," he said, as he stepped in front of Danny, and pushed him aside.

Garda Kelley called for order, then cleared his throat. "As you know, I have been investigating this crime since the beginning and I was just about to make an arrest. In fact, I had this case solved for some time now, but was waiting for the proper moment to make an announcement and an arrest."

Garda Kelley moved toward George Pinkerton.

"You can't be taking this nonsense seriously, Donal," said Pinkerton in astonishment.

Garda Kelley turned to Danny. "Thank you for your help, Mr. O'Flaherty. The *Garda Siochana* will handle things from here on."

Danny stood with his arms crossed, smiling.

Garda Kelley moved toward George Pinkerton. "Mr. Pinkerton," Kelly said ceremoniously, "I'm placing you under arrest for the murder—"

"Garda Kelley," Danny intervened. "May I have a few more words?"

Kelley looked at him. "I think you've interfered with my investigation quite enough, Mr. O'Flaherty."

"Just a few more words."

"Oh, all right."

Danny stood behind the table and waited until Garda Kelley and George Pinkerton were seated again. "Yes," he said, "my grandfather was born to the Pinkerton family five months before their legal marriage. To avoid scandal, the child was given to the O'Flaherty family to raise as their own. But the man who sits in front of us now, George Pinkerton, the grandson of Jeremiah Pinkerton the third, knew nothing about this child."

Garda Kelley looked up, dumbfounded. "But—"

Danny raised a hand for silence. "George Pinkerton is no more responsible for the death of Rose Noonan than I am. He knew nothing of this illegitimate child." Danny looked around the room. "But someone else knew."

Danny moved in front of the table and stared at Mona Noonan. "Rose Noonan knew, of course.

That was the information she was going to give me when I came to Ireland. She knew I was looking for my roots and she intended to tell me everything. And you knew, didn't you Mona?'' Danny asked, pointing at her.

Mona Noonan let out a barely audible squeak. "Yes."

"Your mother told you about the child. But you hid the information from me to save me from shame. You wanted me to leave Ireland because you thought I would be ashamed to learn that my grandfather was born out of wedlock, didn't you, Mona?''

"Yes."

"Well, I thank you for your kindness, but your concerns were unnecessary."

Danny looked around the room. "On the night I was poisoned, there were five people at the pub who could have put arsenic in my stout." Danny walked across the room and stood in front of Seamus Larkin. "First, there was our friendly publican, Seamus Larkin."

Larkin looked at Danny as if he had gone mad.

Danny moved to the other side of the pub and stood in front of Liam Flynn. "You were there that night, too, weren't you, Liam?"

"Of course I was," he snapped.

Danny pointed back at Brendan Grady. "Brendan was there.'' He nodded toward Tim Mahoney. ''And Tim Mahoney.

''But there is one man in Ballycara who clearly remembers the child who was born out of wedlock and sent to live in the O'Flaherty home. Let me remind you that last Sunday, my room was broken into and a letter was taken. Of those five people in the pub that day, one of them had been to Shannonside on Sunday to visit Mrs. Slattery. It would not have been hard for him to go upstairs, let himself into my room, and find the letter.''

Danny stood in front of old Peadar MacGreevy, who stared back at him with fixed eyes, smoking a hand-rolled cigarette. ''You knew who my grandfather really was, didn't you, Peadar?''

MacGreevy looked around him with the expression of a cornered fox. His faded blue eyes were rheumy.

''Didn't you?'' Danny persisted.

Peadar MacGreevy nodded solemnly. ''Sure, I knew. 'Twas years ago. I heard the story from my father when I was but a wee lad meself. My father worked for this man's grandfather.'' He pointed to George Pinkerton. ''I was born on the Pinkerton estate five or six years after your grandfather was born. My father took care of the sheep and cattle. He could tell you loads of stories about what went on in that big house. My father wasn't the kind of man to spread around stories, but one night I heard him talking to me mother about me playmate, Dan O'Flaherty, your grandda. Sure we were both lads. I was seven or eight and he was fifteen or so. I heard my father telling my mother that when Jeremiah Pinkerton died, the true heir to the estate should be little Dan O'Flaherty, cause he was the first son, though a bastard child, of Lord Pinkerton.''

Peadar MacGreevy snubbed out his cigarette, reached a shaky hand out for his pint of stout and took a deep drink. ''Sure, you know the way lads are. I started calling your grandda the 'bastard.' He gave me a good beating for it one time, too. Ah, but 'twas years gone, now. I don't think he ever really knew who his parents were. He knew he wasn't the son of Daniel and Mary O'Flaherty, because they told him that Sean was to inherit the farm when they died. But they treated him like one of their own. They baptized him with the name Daniel after his adopted father. But sure, I don't know if they ever told him why he would never inherit the farm.''

Danny felt sorry, in a way, for Peadar Mac-Greevy.

The old man cleared his throat and continued. ''I remember the day your grandda went out to America as if it were yesterday. He'd worked on the Pinkerton place himself, cutting turf, and saved every pound he made so he could afford his passage to New York. Sure, me and the lads got him good and drunk in this very pub the night he left for America. We all gave him what little we could spare to help him along. And sure, before we knew it he was gone. For all these years I thought 'twas the end of it.''

MacGreevy took another long drink of his stout and wiped his lips with the back of his hand. ''Then Rose Noonan told me that you were coming to Ireland. I asked meself, why would the grandson of Daniel P. O'Flaherty be coming over? Sure, I thought, maybe he knows and he's come back to claim Trelawny.''

Danny sat down, as if from exhaustion, and listened in rapt attention to the old man.

''Then when you got here and started asking questions about when your grandda was born, and looking into the records, then I knew you'd come back to lay claim to the estate. Sure, it wasn't for meself that I was worried a-tall. But I've a son in Dublin who works on the docks. And George Pinkerton here, who's a fine man, has promised twenty-five acres of land to me son when I'm dead and gone.''

The old man looked around, as if for support. ''Don't you see? Sure, I had it in me head you'd be taking the estate away, and I'd be dead and me poor Jamie would spend the rest of his life working himself to death in Dublin. He's a right to some of the land, too, after me working an entire lifetime on it.''

A hush had fallen over the pub.

Peadar MacGreevy continued, ''So I went to Rose Noonan. She knew about your grandda from her ma, and I asked did she intend to tell you about his birth. She said she did, and that it was all over and done with anyway, that there was no way you could take away the estate, even if you wanted to.''

Danny interrupted the tale for the first time. ''Mr. MacGreevy, there is no way I would have wanted to.''

''Sure, and how was I to know? I begged Rose Noonan not to tell you, but she only laughed.'' MacGreevy breathed deeply and let out a sigh. ''The day after you came to the village, I went over to Liam Flynn's house and took a *slane* from the barn.''

Garda Kelly flipped a notebook open on his lap and took notes.

''I went down to Rose's house. I was wearing work gloves and carrying the *slane*. She was in the garden. I begged her not to tell you. I argued with her. When she said she was going to tell you, I...'' Old Peadar MacGreevy started to weep.

Although Danny pitied the old man, he could not put out of his mind, nor forgive, the brutal way in which he had killed Rose—and nearly killed him!

"And so," Danny continued for him, "when she insisted that she was going to tell me the story of my grandfather, you believed that this was going to ruin your son's chances to have a bit of the land. You argued and she resisted. Then, when she turned her back for an instant, you brought the blade of the *slane* down on her head and crushed her skull. You killed her, didn't you?" Danny was shaking with fury and he saw, out of the corner of his eye, Garda Kelley rise.

"Yes," said Peadar MacGreevy sadly. "I killed her."

Danny held out the butt of the hand-rolled cigarette he had picked up beside Rose the day of the murder and laid it next to the butt in front of Peadar MacGreevy. "And you dropped this on your way out."

"This is extraordinary," said George Pinkerton, looking around as if he were lost.

"It is a tragedy," said Danny vehemently. "A senseless, unnecessary tragedy sparked by greed and ignorance."

Garda Kelley took a pair of handcuffs from his belt and moved toward MacGreevy.

"Sure, you hardly need those, Donal," said Peadar MacGreevy wearily. "Aren't I just an old man, with not many days to live?"

"Well, you'll be spending them behind bars,"

said Garda Kelley roughly, as he led Peadar MacGreevy away.

Danny stood in the center of the room as if in shock. Although he was relieved that the ordeal was over, he felt guilty himself. He had come to Ireland to find out who he was. In a way, his arrival had precipitated the murder. But how was he to know that in searching for his roots he would dig up something totally unexpected—a corpse?

The noise of the pub seemed to swirl around him and the events of the past ten days raced through his mind in jumbled, chaotic disorder.

"Drinks on the house," he heard Seamus Larkin call from behind the bar.

Danny smiled, barely able to believe that the old tightwad was loosening up. He glanced at his watch. It was three o'clock. His plane would leave Shannon in three hours.

A jar of Harp appeared in front of him and he sipped it absently. Then he felt a hand on his left shoulder. He turned and looked into the face of Fidelma Muldoon.

"Congratulations, Danny," she said.

Danny nodded wearily. "I wish none of it had ever happened."

"We all do. But what's done is done. 'Twas God's will."

Danny took her hand in his and patted it. "You've been very kind to me, Fidelma." Danny searched for words. "You've been more than kind."

The solemn mood of the pub was changing and Danny could hear the raucous Irish voices rising around him.

"Fidelma," he began again, haltingly. "I feel very close to you in more than a friendly way." He looked into her eyes. "I'd like you to come to New York at Christmas…" He stuttered, searching for words.

"Danny," she said quietly, "I'm afraid you've another surprise in store for you."

Danny laughed nervously. "My God. No more surprises."

Fidelma handed him a photocopied document. "I think you should have a look at this."

Danny took the piece of paper and looked at it, puzzled. It was a copy of a birth certificate. Danny looked up at her. "What…?"

"Just read."

It was Fidelma Muldoon's birth certificate. She was born in Dublin in 1962 to John Muldoon— Danny looked at her again and back at the document—and Elizabeth Pinkerton.

"They're separated now," said Fidelma. "Elizabeth Pinkerton is George's oldest daughter. Of course, there's no divorce in Ireland, so she just left him years ago. But I'm more my father's daughter than my mother's. My father was a Catholic and the Pinkertons disowned Ma when she married him.''

Danny looked at her, dumbfounded. ''This means…'' Danny was still trying to work it all out in his mind. ''We're second cousins, or something.''

Fidelma smiled.

Danny put his head in his hands. ''Oh, no! Did you know about my grandfather, too?''

''Not until just now.'' Fidelma looked at him wistfully. ''I'm sorry.''

''Sorry?''

''I fancied you, Danny,'' she said simply. ''And now it turns out we're related.''

''Fidelma, it doesn't matter,'' said Danny, holding her hand.

''I think it's best not, Danny.''

Danny shook his head and stared at the document. ''Reminds me of what an uncle of mine used to say about the Irish.''

''What's that?''

Danny put on his brogue. ''Sure, we're as mixed up as the dog's breakfast.''

Fidelma burst out laughing.

Suddenly the noise of the pub seemed to shatter their intimacy. Someone had gotten out a *bodhran,* Brendan Grady played a tin-whistle, and Tim Mahoney a fiddle. Danny sat back as the music and laughter swirled around him. Liam Flynn came up and pumped his hand.

"When you coming back, Danny?" Johnny Duffey shouted.

"Next summer," he shouted back.

"Well, you've a home here, sure."

The afternoon passed in a clash of laughter, music and Guinness. Brendan Grady volunteered to drive Danny to the airport and return the rental car. Danny, who swayed slightly from the drink, was grateful. He ran across the street to gather his bags, said goodbye to Mrs. Slattery, and returned to the pub.

The party was in full swing and Danny drank another Harp as he said goodbye to Tim Mahoney, Liam Flynn, and Johnny and Mickey Duffey. Father O'Malley dropped in briefly to bid him farewell, and even George Pinkerton shook his hand.

When Pinkerton had left, Brendan Grady said, "Sure, if it was me, I'd take the Pinkerton estate and send the lot of them packing."

Tim Mahoney doubted, legally, if Danny had any claim to the place at all.

As Brendan and Tim argued about it Danny intervened. "What you fail to realize," he said, "is that I wouldn't want that house or that land. Because these," and Danny spread his hands out to indicate the pub and everyone in it, "these are my people."

"Hear, hear," cried Brendan.

The band struck up a lively tune and the stout flowed. But suddenly the pub became hushed as Fidelma Muldoon rose. All eyes turned to her as she whispered something to Tim Mahoney, who nodded, and quickly tuned his fiddle.

Fidelma took a deep breath. The room was so quiet you could hear her breathing as Tim Mahoney began a slow, sensual introduction and Fidelma launched into song.

*"Oh, Danny Boy, the pipes the pipes are calling*
*From glen to glen, and down the mountain side,*
*The summer's gone and all the roses falling.*
*It's you, it's you must go and I must bide."*

She had a sweet soprano voice, and her lips sensuously kissed each note as she released it. Her eyes were fixed on some point in space as the crowd in the pub looked on, spellbound.

Liam Flynn had a pint of Guinness raised halfway to his lips and held it there as Fidelma Muldoon continued:

*"But come ye back when summer's in the*
*meadow,*
*Or when the valley's hushed and white with*
*snow,*

*It's I'll be here in sunshine or in shadow*
*Oh, Danny Boy, Oh Danny Boy, I love you so.''*

The pub was still as death and all eyes were riveted to Fidelma. Her voice quivered slightly as she went into the second stanza of the song. She flicked her eyes quickly at Danny, who held his jar of Harp against his chest. His eyes were glittering in the light over the bar as he watched her.

*"But when ye come, and all the flowers are*
*  dying,*
*If I am dead, as dead I well may be,*
*Ye'll come and find the place where I am lying,*
*And kneel and say an Ave there for me;*

*And I shall hear, though soft you tread above*
*  me,*
*And all my grave will warmer, sweeter be,*
*For you will bend and tell me that you love me,*
*And I shall sleep in peace until you come to*
*  me!''*

There was an interval of silence as Fidelma's voice cracked. Danny's eyes were gleaming with moisture and then, suddenly, the entire room burst into applause.

Tim Mahoney struck up a lively Irish reel as Brendan led Danny out of the pub, threw his bags into the boot of the car, and turned onto the main road of the village.

"We're late," said Brendan, gunning the engine. "You don't want to miss your plane."

Danny watched as Ballycara disappeared behind them in the rear-view mirror.

"I wouldn't mind," he said.

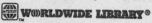

# Take 2 books and a surprise gift FREE!

## SPECIAL LIMITED-TIME OFFER

# AUDITION for Murder

## A MORGAN TAYLOR MYSTERY

### Susan Sussman with Sarajane Avidon

Leave it to diva Lily London to steal the show by dying during struggling actress Morgan Taylor's audition. Okay, so being upstaged by a corpse has its perks—at least she might get a callback.

Then another corpse takes center stage, and things are getting…dramatic, especially when a killer decides it's time to make Morgan's next curtain call her last.

*Available June 2000 at your favorite retail outlet.*

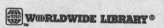 **WORLDWIDE LIBRARY®**

Visit us at www.worldwidemystery.com WSS351

According to *Armchair Detective*,
"If you like Mary Higgins Clark, you'll love…"

# MEG O'BRIEN

High on a hill overlooking the pristine town of
Carmel, California, the body of world-famous
photojournalist Marti Bright is found one morning,
crucified on a wooden cross. For her best friend, Abby
Winthrup, it's just the beginning of a nightmare that
she, too, may not escape from alive.

On sale mid-May 2000 wherever paperbacks are sold!

MMO586

# AILEEN SCHUMACHER

## A TORY TRAVERS/DAVID ALVAREZ MYSTERY

# FRAME WORK FOR DEATH

When a ceiling collapses in an El Paso home, two dead women and a baby are pulled from the wreckage in what at first seems to be a bizarre accident. But to engineer Tory Travers and detective David Alvarez, when a secret room is discovered and the strange connection between the victims emerges, it begins to look suspiciously like murder.

Armed with her code books, calipers and clipboards, Tory determines the means of the murder, and Alvarez uncovers the motive, as a surprising twist, strange revelations and an unlikely killer create a solid framework for death.

*Available May 2000 at your favorite retail outlet.*

WORLDWIDE LIBRARY®

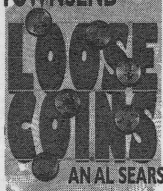